SAPIENCE

A COLLECTION OF SCIENCE FICTION SHORT STORIES

ALEXIS LANTGEN

WWW.LUNARIANPRESS.COM

D1316730

This book is a work of fiction. All the names, places, characters, and incidents are products of the author's lively imagination. Any resemblance to actual events, place, or people living or dead, is entirely coincidental.

For my beautiful family—Anwen, Garren, David, and Mom.

You are my light in dark places.

TABLE OF CONTENTS

CHRYSALIS

Astrogeologist Karen Maguire was giving Commander Harper a status report when her planet hopper started shaking and spinning like a rickety amusement park ride. She'd held on to her seat and gritted her teeth against motion sickness until the hopper smacked into the ice with a bone-shattering jolt.

She typed a command into the keyboard. No response. Static buzzed over the radio, and her console screen had gone black.

What had knocked her out of the frigid Europan sky? Radiation spike from Jupiter? Possible, but the hopper's computers had enough shielding to protect them from all but the most powerful ion bursts. Meteor? She didn't see any holes or dents in the hopper's interior, but there might be damage on the outer hull.

Maguire pushed the console aside and rubbed her temples, thinking. Without a functional computer, she'd have to assess the hopper's location and condition by sight. She opened the emergency locker above the manual controls and pulled out a heavy space suit with a leaded visor. It would give her a minimal amount of protection from the cosmic radiation that streamed over Europa like the invisible currents of a raging river. If she stayed outside the hopper for more than a couple of hours, her hair would start falling out by the handful.

She could stay inside and wait for rescue. But she couldn't be sure the hopper had transmitted her location data before the console went haywire. If the transmission had been interrupted, they'd have no idea where to look for her--she'd been surveying the vast uncharted ice floes that radiated out from the colony, hundreds of miles away from the nearest station. And without access to the meticulously collected data stored on her on-board computer, she didn't know where she'd landed either. She could be deep in an ice crevice, impossible to see. Or she could be in a "soft spot" on the moon's surface, slowly disappearing into a sinkhole of slush and mud.

She slipped into the space suit and pulled the darkened visor over her head. She could barely see while she was inside the hopper, but it would protect her vision from ice blindness. For a while. She opened the escape hatch and took a deep breath to calm her nerves. Even from here, she could see deep dents in the ship's outer hull, though no breaches. She shimmied down the hatch, careful to avoid tearing her suit on the narrow opening. Her thick, insulated boots scraped against solid ice. She let out a sigh of relief--she doubted she would have been able to swim through a slush pit without a dozen blood worms burrowing into her suit.

Maguire studied her surroundings. A mountain of ice crested over her and her ship like a frozen wave. It was not a part of the landscape she'd surveyed, and she had never seen it on any of the other astrogeologists' maps either. Based on the ring-shaped ice formations, Karen figured she was at the bottom of an ancient crater. Her brow furrowed, and she clanked her glove against the visor, forgetting for moment that she couldn't thoughtfully rub her chin while encased in a spacesuit.

She turned back to the hopper. The craft was squat and ungainly on the ground, like a fat metal bullfrog. The rear thrusters had crumpled against the ice. Jagged bits of metal hoses protruded obscenely from the propulsion jumpers. She frowned. No way the craft was going anywhere, and she only had enough emergency supplies for a few days. A week, if she purified and drank some of the Europan ice melt despite its ion contamination.

Karen took a last look at the rugged landscape before she climbed back into the ruined hopper. Jupiter loomed over the sky like a brilliant, multicolored sun, and crystalline shards of ice reflected the great planet's colors in a shimmering array. The view was as stunning as it was the day she'd first arrived on Europa. She'd been a young scientist eager to prove herself, awed and terrified at the same time. Then, as now, she put on a brave face and kept going, even when the first life systems failed her first year, and they'd had to spend weeks constructing a new water filtration system from scratch.

She spent the next few days repairing her radio and looking for ways to boost its signal out of the crater. There was nothing to eat but stale protein bars from the emergency kit, but they kept her going. She hated being stuck in the cramped hopper but didn't dare spend too much time in the cosmic radiation. If she had to walk somewhere to get a better signal, she couldn't risk getting over exposed before she left.

Despite building a longer antenna from the salvaged remains of the thrusters, the radio silence continued. Worse-

-she'd activated the hopper's rescue beacon in hopes of getting a ping from one of the satellites but got nothing.

She couldn't have fallen that far off course. Based on her memories of the crash, the hopper couldn't be more than fifty miles outside of her planned trajectory. Between the radio and the beacon, she should have had a signal by now. Or a rescue party from the domes.

There was something strange of about the crash itself, too. The hopper's rockets had been purring along just fine, then wham! The diagnostic programs should have caught a malfunction, and the atmospheric scanners should have warned her about incoming meteors or radiation spikes.

Scanners could fail, of course. Worse, they could be tampered with. The colonists were a close-knit bunch and they trusted each other but living so far from Earth's comforts could take a toll on someone's mental stability. And the colony was not immune to Earth's complicated geopolitics--she knew that the United Federation and the Pacific League had frequent spats over Europa's land and mineral rights. It was possible to sabotage the colony from Earth, if someone had the right equipment.

And if whatever hit her had damaged the colony's biodomes...

She shivered. Thousands of people lived in the colony, not just the handful of scientists and pilots they'd had in the beginning. Families started arriving as soon as they'd finished the second biodome. Her brother worked in the botany department of Dome II with his wife, and she was seven months pregnant. Their baby would be the eighth one born at the colony in the last five years. Karen had joked they should name her "Octavia."

She had to focus. She was running out of time. Though she hadn't left the hopper in days, the Geiger counter in her visor had been flashing dire warnings at her for the last twelve hours. The hopper's hull had to have a breach somewhere she couldn't reach. But where could she go? She couldn't climb out of the crater.

The signal. The ice blocked it from traveling in most directions. But if she got to the center of the crater, far from the ice walls, she could broadcast in a wider array and have a better chance of contacting a satellite. But traveling any distance over the exposed ice would be terribly dangerous, practically a suicide mission.

Maguire ran a hand through her hair, which was matted and stringy from days of neglect. A thick clump came loose in her fingers. She clutched the greasy, dull strands in her fist. I won't die here, she told herself, stuck in this twisted hunk of metal. I'll die on my feet.

She gathered everything she needed into the emergency parachute she'd fashioned into a makeshift bag and slipped on her spacesuit. Then she shimmied down the escape hatch and onto the ice. Jupiter hung in the sky, in the exact place it had the last time she'd gotten out of the hopper, a perfect landmark.

And a treacherous king, she thought. The tumultuous planet took after its namesake, the philandering god. It had chaotic weather patterns, inscrutable geography, and sent bursts of debris and radiation hurtling towards its satellites with terrible abandon. It bore down on Europa, looming over her landscape until the ice sparkled in reflected reds and oranges. The red spot glared at Karen like a giant eye, pulsing with fury.

She took a deep breath through the condenser module on her suit--it could pull in enough oxygen from Europa's atmosphere that she didn't need tanks. She bent into a low crouch, then launched herself into the air. Even in the bulky suit and carrying an unwieldy bag, she soared upwards, the low gravity allowing her to leap like a weird space cricket. Her boots crunched against crystalline glaciers as she landed.

Karen peered back at the hopper, tucked beneath icy cliffs like a toad in a hole. She estimated she'd jumped a little over a hundred feet. Not far enough. She jumped a few more times, then pulled out the radio. Setting it up took longer than she liked, but she didn't dare rush--the thick padding of her suit made her fingers awkward and clumsy, and the intense cold made them numb. She hunched over the antenna, breathing slow and deep to combat waves of dizziness and nausea. Signs of radiation poisoning. By the time she finished, she could feel dry itchiness spreading over her back. She wondered if her skin was peeling away.

Focus, Karen told herself. She turned the radio on and adjusted it to the widest possible set of frequencies. Nothing. She lifted the antenna over her head, slowly turning it in hopes of picking up a signal, any signal.

What was that? When she pointed the antenna towards the center of the crater, the radio crackled and moaned. It wasn't any beacon she'd ever heard before, but it was something. She narrowed the incoming frequencies to clear it up.

She heard thumping, gurgling sounds, like a heartbeat underwater. Karen sucked in her breath. A memory swelled in her brain. Doctor's office. Stirrups. Images on a screen, fuzzy and indistinct. Listening to her daughter's heartbeat on an ultrasound for the first time. Where was Hannah now? She flew reconnaissance missions to Jupiter and its other moons and was scheduled to explore Ganymede for the next few weeks.

Karen pushed those thoughts aside. Whatever signal the radio picked up, it was her only shot now. It might be an abandoned outpost, or the remains of a crashed ship from the early days. Whatever it was might have food, shelter, and old parts she could use to further boost her emergency beacon.

She gathered the radio into her parachute bag and started jumping. Each leap left her breathless and sick. After the third one she vomited into her regulator. Her vision grew so blurry she didn't see the crack until she'd nearly landed on it--a crevice in the ice, its sides steep.

Maguire looked over the side. About fifteen feet down, the translucent ice gave way to rocky brown. She frowned. Europa didn't have rocks beneath the ice, only a silvery green ocean. But the ocean was hundreds of feet deep--this must be something else, a rock that lodged in the ice but didn't penetrate. The rock looked hollow, like a cave millions of miles from where it should be.

Should she tumble down the rabbit hole? If she stayed up here, she'd die, probably in a matter of hours. She'd freeze and burn at the same time. Yet she knew they'd discovered creatures on Europa, big ones. Ones that could eat her, tear her apart.

At least it'd be quick, she thought, her curiosity defeating her fear. She slipped her legs over the end of the crevice one at a time, lowering herself down until she could drop. She expected to feel solid rock under her feet when she landed, but she didn't. The brown substance had a spongy feel instead. A type of plant, maybe? If she ever got home, she'd have to show it to her brother.

She peered into the cave. It was lined with blue-green soft fronds that reminded her of corals or sea anemones. They gave off a gentle bioluminescent glow. Her chest ached at their delicate beauty. No one had ever discovered anything like this. Not that it mattered--she'd likely die before she could show it to anyone. Her head swirled.

I might as well carry on, she thought. Maybe the fronds would dissolve her body for food after she died. She hoped her carcass wouldn't contaminate them with radiation.

She wandered further down the tunnel, fronds brushing against her legs. Her nausea and exhaustion faded away, and she felt warm for the first time in days. After a few hundred feet, she saw something hanging from the top of the cave, like an enormous pupa. She hesitated, expecting to feel trepidation or reluctance, yet she felt calm, even joyful, as though she was coming home.

Why did it feel so welcoming? Pheromones? Or had she lost fear in the face of her impending death? She could feel bald patches forming on her scalp where clumps of her hair fell out. Even away from the radiation, she was too poisoned now to survive.

Karen approached the chrysalis. It reached from the top of the cave to the bottom, perhaps about ten feet long. It was a semi-translucent golden brown and gave off a faint glow from the inside. The outer shell felt firm, but flexible, and it pulsed slightly under her fingers. She yearned to take off her suit and touch it with her bare skin.

A mad, suicidal thought, she realized. The sickness must be affecting her mind. It was warm enough in the cave that she didn't need the insulation and deep enough to protect her from the radiation, but Europa had so little atmospheric pressure taking off her glove would be dangerous. But the seams in her suit were tight enough to keep most of it pressurized if she only took off one glove. If the anemones were going to attack her, they probably would have done it by now. And she was already dying.

She unlatched one of her suit's gloves and pulled off the stiff, leaded fabric. The skin on her hand was red and peeling. Her knuckles had painful cracks covered in dry, black blood. The air inside the cave felt good though--higher humidity and more air pressure than she'd expected. She ran a trembling finger along the chrysalis. It was as smooth as fine-woven silk. The pulsing grew, and she could see movement behind the translucent shell.

Karen drew back. The chrysalis shook, and a seam opened along the top. A thin appendage emerged, but she couldn't tell whether it was a leg or something like an insect antenna, or something else entirely. Whatever it was, it had the shiny iridescence of a butterfly's wing in midnight blue and deep purple.

She stared at it, rooted to the spot. Fear raced through her veins, but it wasn't the sickening fear of danger. It was the heady exhilaration of discovery. Something momentous lay before her, something new and strange and wonderful. Something as terrifying and risky as all things new and strange and wonderful are. She took a deep breath to steady herself.

The appendage waved. It had the suppleness of a tentacle, but it was covered in a jointed shell. It curled and uncurled, then seemed to beckon.

But that was ridiculous. How could an alien understand human gestures? She had learned enough astrobiology to know to be wary of misinterpreting potential contacts with alien organisms. She had no idea what level of intelligence this creature possessed, much less what its gestures meant. And yet...

The tentacle (feeler? antennae?) seemed to inspect her. It circled in Karen's direction, at least, and she noticed a handful raised bumps at its tip, like a sensory node of some kind. The seam in the chrysalis opened further, allowing the tentacle to come close enough to touch her. But it didn't. Instead, the tip of the tentacle opened, like flower petals uncurling as they bloomed. Delicate, feathery fronds trembled in the air near her. Was it picking up her scent, or perhaps emitting a signal of its own, as flowers did?

Entranced, Karen lifted her bare hand, longing to touch it, yet afraid. The creature brushed against her raw skin, its touch light and soft. For the first time, it made a noise, a chirping sound like a dolphin or a cricket. The sound startled her, and she felt herself shaking. Her head throbbed, and bile rose in her throat. How much longer did she have? Not long.

The creature chirped again, and it sounded dismayed. Don't assign it human emotions, she told herself. She had no way of knowing...

Her vision darkened. She blinked. Tears burned as they ran down the blistered, cracked skin on her cheeks. Hannah. She loved her. She'd never see her again.

Karen sank to her knees. The air inside her helmet was too hot, too close. She unlatched her helmet and pushed it off. She leaned her head into the silky chrysalis and felt the feather-light brush of the tentacle fronds against her face. A comforting scent washed over her, like spicy flowers. It smelled like heaven.

Just before she passed out, she felt the tentacle wrap around her abdomen. It lifted her up, taking her inside the chrysalis. She decided she didn't mind it eating her. That much.

She was somewhere warm. There was liquid all around her, but she could still breathe. Dizzy, disoriented. Her skin hurt, and her fingers felt swollen and stiff. There was a humming, throbbing sound in her ears, then a soothing noise like the sound of the sea inside a conch shell. When she opened her eyes, she saw a soft, golden light. It suffused the thick liquid, giving it honey glow. She tried to move. It hurt--her injured skin felt like it split open.

I'm naked, she realized. Her suit was gone. She lightly touched her head. Her hair was gone too, and her bare scalp felt strange and alien. Help, she thought. She tried to scream, but there was something covering her mouth.

A tentacle wrapped around her chest. Karen started to struggle. She could hear a voice whispering inside her head. She couldn't make out distinct words, only images and feelings. Love, kindness. Help.

It seemed to be asking her a question. Her answer was yes.

They sang to each other across the vastness of space. Thousands of travelers spread across the galaxy but always in contact, like a vast neural net. Karen sang with them. She heard them singing back to her, telling her of distant planets, alien stars. She was one of them; she had been welcomed into their community with a ritual exchange of genetic material and a quantum entanglement.

The one who had welcomed her held her in a gentle embrace. This one was wise and old, and it told her of its eons floating in the chrysalis, from star to star, sharing its genes. It puzzled that her body was so ill-equipped to survive on Europa. The youngest one--for that was how they thought of Karen, the newest member of their tribe--explained about Earth, in halting songs and subtle electrical waves. The wise one laughed. To travel the stars in metal cocoons, without properly altering oneself for survival! How strange.

But it was no matter. Wise One enjoyed the challenge of repairing and strengthening the youngest one's fragile body. She could survive on the icy moon now, Wise One told her, and live on Earth again if she chose to return.

There are others, Youngest One sang. My daughter.

Fear not. I will teach you to weave the chamber and leave the Ceriantharia here to produce silk. Then you may give others the gifts I've given you.

So Youngest One sang of joy, until the time of parting came. Wise One stroked her progeny's head, which was now the same lustrous blue as the Wise One's tentacles.

Go in Peace, Wise One sang to her. Bring my gifts to the people of your birth.

Youngest One clung to Wise One's thorax, and water leaked from her eyes. I will miss you, she sang. Where will you go?

I will go to the stars. It is my purpose to exchange greetings with the children of the universe and bring them into our family. Do not mourn, Youngest. I will sing to you always, across time and space.

Youngest One nodded and touched the center of her chest, where the entangled particles were embedded. She released Wise One and stepped back.

Wise One made the gesture of loving farewell with both tentacles. As part of the final motions, the alien clasped a net, carefully woven from hundreds of thousands, perhaps millions of thin, reflective silk strands. With a motion perfected by eons of repetition, Wise One hurled the net into the air. It caught on the faint winds of Europa and floated into the sky, spreading into a wide sail. Wise One's outer shell cracked, releasing a tiny egg-shaped inner core.

Youngest watched Wise One's core drift away--first across Europa's sky, then, as the sail caught more solar radiation, out into space itself. Wise One sang to her of the freedom and joy of travel, of the pleasures of weaving a new chrysalis suitable for deep space. The journey might take a thousand years or more, but then Wise One would find a suitable planet or a moon or even a comet. It would have life, or it would evolve life. Wise One would wait patiently, listening to the songs of her many children, until the life approached. Then they would exchange genetic material and entangle their particles, and the family would grow.

When she could no longer see Wise One on the horizon, Youngest One gathered the leftover exoskeleton and carefully brought it down into the cave. She arranged it inside the remains of the chrysalis where she had undergone her transformation. She felt it was the right way to honor and preserve the physical manifestation of the Wise One's visit to the Jovian moon.

When she was done, Youngest gathered silk from the Ceriantharia, and she began to weave. She did not yet have the skill to catch the light of the sun in a great sail, but she could make a smaller weave, one that would allow her to ride the air currents of Europa's thin atmosphere. When she'd finished, she had gossamer wings that stretched out from her arms for several meters. She climbed out of the cave with exquisite care, but the silk was as strong as it was light, and the wings did not tear.

She stood on the precipice of the cave she'd once climbed into, sick and dying. Jupiter hung in the sky, enormous, seething with terrible beauty. But now the radiation did not burn her skin, and she could breathe the cold air without pain or struggle. Indeed, the frozen terrain felt light and pleasant, the shards of ice like grass beneath her feet.

Youngest One lifted her wings, and they caught the air. She floated into the sky. Stretching her new-made limbs to their fullest, she swam through the air, diving and swooping with sheer jubilation. From up high, she could see the crushed hopper. It felt like she'd crawled out of it ages ago, but only a thin film of ice covered the metal frame. She marveled that only a few weeks had past, at most. In the distance, she saw the twinkling lights of a tiny outpost from the colony. She wondered if they had been looking for her, and what they would make of her when they saw her. But she did not wonder long--it was time to go back. They needed her, whether they knew it or not. So, with a graceful arc, Karen returned to the people of her birth.

DEEP ICE

Mother never stopped talking about the Selkie Unit. She told me the stories over and over again, until I'd learned them all by heart. She told them to my father and his friends, who smiled awkwardly as she repeated herself, swirling their drinks and searching for an escape. Her friends had all vanished beneath the ice of Europa on their last mission, a dangerous bid to repair cracks in the colony's foundation.

She talked so much about the unit that the colony director gave her a job teaching water safety and submersion protocols to new arrivals, where she could talk about it to people who hadn't heard it all before.

It was a joke of course, a condescending pat on the head for a woman who'd been their leading scientist, a pioneer in the study of an alien ocean. New arrivals didn't even need to know submersion protocols because no one swam in the deep seas anymore. They sent drones when they bothered to explore at all, which wasn't often. But mother never let up. It hurt to listen to her.

"The suits were key, Chaya," she said to me. "We engineered their padded linings from billions of nanotube

15

matrices. They could withstand enormous pressure and extreme temperatures. Each suit was keyed to its user's DNA to provide them with a complex array of supports: breathing, hormone and neurotransmitter regulation, temperature regulation, food provision, and waste removal. The protein analysis and replication unit alone was one of the most brilliant pieces of tech I've ever seen! We could go on missions in the deep seas for days, even months on end."

She had such confidence in the suits that long after the funerals she remained convinced her old team had survived somewhere in the deep and frigid waters. No one had come back from that last mission alive.

"The discoveries--it's unbelievable to me even now, but we saw it. Bioluminescent reefs, beautiful and strange beyond anything on Earth. Quadropi, with their long tentacles and bright, ever changing colors. Leila was convinced the color changes represented a primitive language. She was tracking the quadropi's migratory patterns to help us decipher it. Phil..."

I tuned her out.

"Your mother was a hero," Father said when she wasn't around. His shoulders slumped, and each word sounded like it was being dragged out of his mouth. "But her missions terrified me. She'd go down into that deep, black hole drilled in ice a mile thick. I felt like it was swallowing her up. And what would happen to us if she never came home? I can't live without her. I never told her, but I was relieved when her suit was damaged. Gwydion built those, and no one could repair them once he was gone. Although someday maybe you could, kiddo." He smiled then and patted my shoulder the way he always did when he remembered my gift for tech. I had long since figured out how to repair basic colony systems, and I'd picked up some advanced stuff from mother.

Father worked in the AgTech labs on the upper levels of the colony, as far from the dark waters as he could get. He'd tried to get mother to work there, too, but she had no interest in soil samples and seed genomes.

"It's a waste of a brilliant mind," he complained about her water safety job. "You have a doctorate in astrobiology, Becca! Don't let it all go because you're holding on to the past."

On the good days, she'd agree with him. On those days she'd teach me about the complicated chemical interactions in an ecosystem, or she'd experiment with ways to make our rations of dehydrated, powdered foods into something delicious. But the deep oceans always called her back.

"The quadropi, the glow coral, the pulse of the deep vents themselves, they had a rhythm, a song almost, and you could hear it while you were there, these...harmonies. It's like nothing I've seen or heard of on Earth. Even now, even on the base, I can almost hear it. And sometimes in my dreams, I can hear them, too, the others from the deep unit," she told me one night. She was in my room stroking my hair while I was suffering a bad bout of colony crud. She must have thought I asleep or too feverish to hear her properly, because she'd never mentioned anything about the reefs "singing" ever before.

"The glow corals sing?" I'd murmured.

"Of course not, it's a metaphor, and... go to sleep."

She didn't talk about it again, but her words stayed with me. I worried about her, like my father did when he wasn't pretending everything was fine.

As the years passed, her obsession grew. She pulled out her old suit, running her hands over the twining nanotubes, explaining the buttons and dials to me or anyone else who'd listen. I caught her wearing it when I came home early from school one day. She had her eyes closed and she swayed back and forth, as though moving in an an invisible current. She didn't hear me or open her eyes when I came in, and watching her reverie felt almost indecent or obscene, as though I'd walked in on her nude or doing something intimate. I backed out of the living module and went back to one of the common areas until it was time for my father to come home.

Dinner that night was quiet, but something raw and heavy hung over our kitchenette.

"The power core," mother whispered. In the silence her words echoed through our module like quiet scream. "Someone drained it. The lines were cut. I hadn't noticed that before."

"You must have had an accident on the reef," father said. He kept his head down on the protein crumbles in front of him. Mother had rolled them into balls in imitation of his favorite Earth food--Italian meatballs--but they had come undone in the thin, acidic tomato sauce.

"No," mother said, quieter now. "I would have died, if it had broken then. It was tampered with, before the last mission. That's why I couldn't go. That's why I couldn't save them."

"You couldn't have saved them," father said. "You need to stop telling yourself that. There was nothing you could have done, and you were pregnant, and you had no business--"

"They didn't have a full team." mother said, her breath ragged. "They didn't have the support they needed."

"You would have died, too," he said.

"I wouldn't have been alone."

"I would have been alone, without you. Forever."

"You always hated me. You despised the things I loved."

18

"I loved you. I wanted you. I wanted our child, our love, our marriage. I wanted safety and peace and..."

"You wanted a lie."

Silence. I froze in my chair.

Mother let out a shuddering breath. Her eyes filled with tears.

"I can't," she said. "I'm sorry."

I heard the scrape of a chair and her arms folded around me. Softness. She wailed, and her face was wet. I wanted to sink into her embrace. I wanted to hold her and wipe the tears off her face. I wanted to shove her and hear the thud of her body hitting the floor. But I froze, as cold and motionless as the mountains of ice that surrounded the colony on the surface above.

When I came home from school the next day, I found her curled up on the floor of her room. There were pictures, real pictures on the photo paper the colony had run out of years ago, scattered on the floor around her. I bend to pick them up, careful not to bend the edges or damage something so rare and precious. What could be worth a physical picture?

Her team. I recognized them from the memorial videos they played on the anniversary of the tragedy. The pictures weren't stiff or formal, the way most physical pictures were. These were--spontaneous. Mom, younger, her face lit up with a smile, her arm wrapped around the neck of her best friend, Leila Hassan. Dr. Hassan smiled too, and she was raising a sculpted glass of dark red liquid, like blood.

"Were you testing samples?" I asked, holding up the picture. "What kind of extractor is that?"

Mother pushed curtain of hair away from her face. "Those are wine glasses. It's for a kind of drink we had on Earth. We don't have it here."

19

"I've heard of it," I said. "If these aren't documentation, why do you have a physical picture?"

"It's from before we left Earth," she said. She turned away, and her voice was muffled by the floor. "It was the day we finished our Europan training. We were celebrating, and we took these. I brought them with me when we came." She sounded tired and old, so old. When had she gotten so old?

"Oh," I said.

"I won't see her again," mother said. "None of them." She picked up one of the pictures and touched the faces. They were all smiling, laughing. I couldn't remember the last time I'd ever seen her like that. If I'd ever seen her like that.

"I know," I said.

"The worst...worst...I'll never know what happened to them. If there was anything I could have done. If they...suffered."

"I'm sorry, mom."

"And the oceans--the amazing oceans--the discoveries. It's all gone. Everything they--we--worked for."

"I wish I could help," I said.

"No one can help," she said. "But I love you for caring. No one else does. Not anymore." She sat up. I took her hand and helped her stand.

"What should I do now?" she asked, raking her hands through her hair.

"I don't know."

She stopped going to her water safety job after that. She didn't leave the module much. A representative of the colony director came to try to assign her to another job. She stared straight ahead as he spoke and didn't say a word until he left. There was talk of sending her back to Earth for "treatment," but colony resources were always stretched thin. Return vessels were needed to export the rare minerals the colony mined, not ferry maddened colonists.

I completed my apprenticeship and advanced in my studies. Mother didn't come to the ceremony. I had leave to study and repair the most advanced equipment and drones.

Her old selkie suit hung in our storage bay, limp and splayed. I touched the nanotube matrices. I'd read about them, but they weren't like any of the other suits in the colony--slimmer and finer than the hardy ice climbers, tougher than the hazmats. Gwydion, the colony's genius engineer, had molded the selkie suits on his own before leaving on a doomed mission to the other outer planets, or so I'd been told. Mother's suit had an elegance of design for something so maddeningly complex, and even twenty years after its creation, its tech remained a cutting-edge mystery.

I found the suit's broken heart, its power core. Several bundles of nanotubes fell away from it, their edges hacked and torn, but the core itself was intact. I knew all the colony's construction supplies and materials--the huge varieties of metal alloys, nanotubes, and advanced polymers we need to maintain the modules and construct all the life-support and exploration equipment. But this was something different. It felt light, even flexible under my hands. It had resisted, or perhaps self-healed, some of the damage my father had inflicted on it when he hacked away its nanos.

The suit had an exterior control panel, and I pressed some of the buttons. It didn't turn on. But as I manipulated its controls, I felt as though something in the power core responded, like the distant stirrings of a deep sleeper. Was it just my imagination? I took a sample of one of the broken nanos for analysis. I considered taking the whole suit, but I didn't want to know how mother would react if she found it gone.

Under the microscope, the suit's nanotech was amazing. Its nanotubes had an interlocking crystalline structure I'd never seen before, and its microbots showed a degree of independence light years ahead of the few I'd studied during my apprenticeship. I spent weeks examining them, but it felt like I'd barely scratched the surface.

One day I came home from the lab to find mother cooking choco-protein biscuits, one of my favorites.

"I know what you're doing," she said, her eyes soft and luminous. She gave me a smile that made me feel warm and safe in a way I hadn't felt in a long time.

"I can't promise anything," I told her.

"You're the most brilliant nanotech engineer in the colony. Far more advanced and creative than those old ice-legs in colony R & D."

I shrugged.

"Just keep trying," she breathed. "Please. I can feel the walls of this place closing in, and the suit is my only way out."

I didn't answer. A thousand thoughts ran through my head, doubts and fears and horrid visions. But also, images of my mother crying for joy, hugging me. My parents happy for the first time I could remember. My mother, a colony hero once more, not the sad joke she'd become.

"I will."

I went back to the lab. This time I brought the whole suit to examine. Fortified by choco-protein, everything seemed easier than it had before. A little spark of electricity, a coat of the right combination of catalysts, and a bit of fuel. The suit's tiny nanobots sprang to life. They swarmed the broken ends of the nanotubes, repairing the severed lines and healing the breach.

I watched them work with endless fascination, their meticulous, microscopic dance, as coordinated as a swarm of bees. It took most of the night, and several different catalysts, and a few large sheets of graphene, but it worked. The suit, mother's beloved suit, was fixed.

I didn't stop to think. I didn't wait for rest to clear my mind, or caution to root itself in my excitement. I cradled the suit in my arms like a precious thing, a beloved gift. I ran to give it to my mother.

Her reaction was everything I hoped. Tears streamed down our faces.

"My brilliant daughter," she said, cradling me in her arms. "I love you so much."

"I fixed it for you," I said. "And we'll be happy now. You can forgive him, and everything will be alright."

"Yes," she said. "Yes, it will."

She wiped her eyes. "We should go test it."

"Sure. The practice pool for the drones is--"

"No, it has to be in the real ocean. The deep sea."

"But...are you sure? It only just started working again, and something could go wrong, or--"

"Oh Chaya, such a worrier! Once it's on, once it's working--they're like magic. Self-healing. Protein replication. It's a miracle!"

"But it wouldn't take that long too--"

"Please! It's been too long already and I'm dying in here. I have to go back!"

Her arms fell away from me and her face twisted, and I didn't want to ruin whatever joy we had now and so I said yes, I'll help you, yes.

And I followed her to the entry point, no one guarded it anymore, because who would go down the black hole, the deep black hole drilled in the ice a mile thick.

She slipped in the suit like it was born to her, like it was a second skin. She kissed me once and said, I love you, Chaya. Maybe someday I'll see you again. And I said, what do you mean? And before I could stop her, she'd clipped on to the lowering cables and disappeared into the dark. Once she was gone, I felt cold all over, as if all warmth had fled with her.

I sat there, by the edge of the abyss, waiting. Waiting. Waiting. Seconds stretched to minutes and hours and what felt like days. And my father found me, huddled by the hole. His face fell and he wept and sobbed.

She's gone, he said. She's gone forever...

I froze. I tried to tell myself she was dead, that the suit hadn't worked after all. I yearned for the sickening sweetness of guilt or raw edge of grief. But I couldn't make myself believe it. Maybe, she'd said. Maybe I'll see you again. Maybe. She didn't want to come back, not now, not ever. She hadn't loved me enough to come back.

But oh, I still loved her, and it hurt. And I wanted to hate her, but I didn't, and I drew schematics and I'm still drawing them. I was the first person in a decade to fix a selkie suit and I'll be the first person since Gwydion to build one, too. And I'll build my own suit and slip down the hole, the pitch-black hole in the deep ice, and I'll go down into the deep oceans and I'll find her.

HUSK

I don't know why I keep coming back to this place. There's nothing here apart from broken lab equipment and leftover parts, everything coated with a fine layer of dust. Nothing lives here anymore, and no one comes here except for rare government auditors, mischievous kids, and me.

But the endoskeletons are intact. Long, slender, flexible, and not a bit of rust. Elegantly designed, if I should say so myself. Not that I designed them, of course, but I chose the designer. What was her name? She had a small round face, owlish glasses, and never spoke above a whisper unless someone fudged her work. After our project went bust, she designed the stilt-suits and planet hoppers they used for mining the asteroid belt. A waste of talent, I thought at the time. In the end though, they paid her a pretty penny, and research is all exo-suits now.

I wrap my scarf around my neck and pull the mylar jacket close. It crinkles. I know I shouldn't, but I light a cigarette. Not an inhaler, a real one, hard to come by these days. I lean against a busted table and pull out a flask. The liquid inside smells like a combination of motor oil and turpentine. Synths

25

haven't done a good job on liquor, not yet, and nothing else is affordable on a low-level researcher's salary. I try not to think too about the times I had hundred-year-old scotch for anniversaries like this, but the memories stir nonetheless. I remember the peaty aroma and the warmth that suffused my limbs as I drank it, but the taste itself eludes me, like so many other things.

There is one face module that's still intact. It hung on the walls of my office once, like a trophy or a piece of art, but I took it down after they destroyed the project. I'd been one of those kids that was forever squirreling things away, hiding my small treasures in places I imagined they'd be safe forever. That must have been why I hid the face. Not in any place particularly brilliant or clever, but in one of those ordinary places no one thinks to look. And sure enough, there it is still today, behind a loose vent in the wall. Dusty, but intact. I wipe the grime off the module with my shirt.

And there he is, or a part of him, Project 759. Without motion or sensors, it looks like he did when he shut down, blank and expressionless. Not cold or inhuman, whatever they said later. Not angry. Just empty.

They chose me to lead the project because of my post-grad work at University, and because I was one of the only advanced hardware developers who could pass the background check for a security clearance (the rest of the geniuses were a rather debauched lot). Can you imagine it now, a postdoc plucked from academic obscurity and given a nearly unlimited research budget? I had the best of everything--teams of designers and coders, a state-of-the-art lab, access to top secret research. All I had to do was build a functioning AI, a goal that had proved elusive despite the many technological breakthrough of the past century.

26

If I'd had a bit less arrogance, I might have glimpsed my fate when I met my predecessor. Sai Gupta had been the golden boy of Harvard and Oxford, a legend in his own time. He'd built his own super-computer at twelve and landed on the cover of Time Magazine at twenty-three. When I'd met him, he was barely thirty, but he'd had the stooped shoulders and red-rimmed eyes of an old man. His hands shook as he handed me the keys to the lab, and his breath reeked.

"Hi, I'm John--"

"I know who you are," he'd cut in. "I'll show you around."

I'd followed him through the lab a like a puppy in a butcher's shop, marveling at the equipment, the designs, the white boards covered in elegant numbers, code, and notes. But as we moved deeper into the building, I noticed other things. A terrible burnt smell. Broken beer bottles. Mildewed dampness beneath dripping emergency showers. And on the last door, dried black stains that looked like blood.

"It's in here," he said. "What's left of it." He typed a complex code into the final door, then pushed it open.

I held my breath, then let it out in a disappointed sigh. It was only a plain gray box, with vents like an ordinary computer. But there were holes burned in its sides, and two crushed robotic arms heaped in a corner.

"Jesus," I said. "What the hell happened here? What's with the burns?"

Sai gave a harsh laugh. "That's classified, my friend. But take my advice. Don't build yours in a box. It makes them angry." He ran his hand over the box, his expression unreadable. After a long moment, he stumbled back towards the door. "Let's get out of here."

Before I left the lab that day, he gave me a bottle of scotch.

27

"It's a hundred years old," he said. "I bought it for the day...never mind. It's yours now, Dr. Mathis. Congratulations."

"Thanks," I said. "And I'll take your advice. No box."

He gave me a strained smile. "It was shitty advice. I should have told you to run for the fucking door and never come back."

I never saw Sai again. A few weeks later someone found him washed up on a beach near Montecito. The news reported it was an accident. At the time, I wanted to believe that.

Some people might wonder why we chose to give an AI emotion at all. In the aftermath of our failures, plenty of people asked that, including some irate congressmen at a classified congressional hearing. But it doesn't work that way.

Imagine any kind of living creature, even a simple one like a bacterium. That bacterium has needs, and in a primitive way, desires. It needs to find nutrients, reproduce, avoid predators. I'm not saying it's conscious, at least not in the same way we are, but it's motivated. When scientists tried to make an AI without emotions, they didn't have any motivation--no desire, no fear. Nothing. And that's what it did--nothing. No communication, no creativity, no non-linear thinking. They weren't any different from any other super-computer, so far as anyone could tell. Conscious thought, which after all originated in emotional organic beings, required emotion to work.

Or so we thought anyway--maybe by now someone else has figured out consciousness without emotions. But if they have, that's news to me.

Anyway, when I took over the project, I got to read the previous researchers' notes. The first researchers programmed models with only "good" emotions--joy, pleasure, contentment. Their AIs would interact with humans a little bit at first, but the machines quickly learned that they'd feel good no matter what. The blissful bastards spent most of their time completely immobile but for the peaceful smile on their faces. The project manager noted with increasing frustration that no one could get enough information from the bliss bots to see if they passed the Turing test. Every time a human talked to them, they'd say things like "I am awake" and "Be free from fear and attachment" until everyone wanted to punch them right in their stupid serenely smiling faces. In the end, all of them were scrapped for parts.

After the bliss bots, the next program head decided to give the AIs fear and sadness, and even a touch of anger. She even programmed behavioral controls into the emotion protocols, so the Projects would feel joy when they pleased the researchers and sadness or fear when they didn't. But the lack of emotional flexibility left them with AIs that acted like weird robotic dogs. They jumped through any hoops the researchers gave them but didn't know or care why. They became so slavish they had meltdowns any time researchers tried to get them to think independently. Literally--there were scorch marks on the floor. Eventually, they were re-programmed and uploaded into a fluffy children's toys. They had a brief burst of popularity one Christmas, then disappeared from the market when kids grew bored with the world's clingiest robot pets.

Sai went a different direction with his research. He wanted his AI to be passionate about justice and have a strong sense of right and wrong. It didn't work out like he'd hoped.

I like to think I came closest, in the end. Not that it mattered.

I had the lab rebuilt to make it more "Zen." Soft lighting, small fountains, pots of bamboo, the works. I scrapped most of the hardware designs that Sai had made but kept most of his code. I had alterations made in a few key points, of course--toning down Project 759's ability to feel anger or outrage, for instance. And it was my idea to get a surrogate in here. Not a sex surrogate, no matter what those prurient idiots in the press said. A relationship surrogate--Danu.

I'd first met her in college, when she still called herself Danny, or even Daniela if she felt like it. She smelled like patchouli and cloves, and her hair back then was long and tangled and curly. She wasn't my type, or so I thought at the time, but there was something about her that drew me. Warmth, maybe, or the soft curves she had even when all the other girls on campus took Thinspiration pills until they resembled a horde of starving peasants. I never dated her, but our orbits crossed often enough. There was one night, I was depressed I'd gotten rejected by one girl or another, and I found myself in her room. I remember her holding me while I cried and vomited in her bathroom. Then she'd wrapped her pillowy arms around me and let me rest my head on her chest. Before that moment, I'd never felt cared for, truly loved. A week later, she sheared off her hair as part of a campus protest. The dean had her and the other protesters arrested to crack down on radicalism, and I didn't see her again for a long time.

But being the program manager of a secret and prestigious project has its advantages. With my access to government networks and my security clearance, I'd found her. They'd kept her in a minimum security "trust" house, comfortable confinement for someone accused of subverting established order. When they brought her to me, she wasn't even wearing incapacitator cuffs, only a monitor embedded under her skin.

30

"Danny!" I'd said when we met again, around the time my team had completed our first prototype. "I missed you."

She blinked at first and didn't answer. One of the agents who'd accompanied her gave her a sharp nudge. She twitched a bit then nodded. "Good to see you, too, John. And I call myself Danu now."

"Danu, then. Has anyone told you about the project?"

"No," she answered, her eyes staring distantly.

"Well, it's my theory that the reason we've failed for so long with AI is poor socialization. I mean, they may not be organic creatures, but they need to understand how organics live and function, or they'll be too alien to want to do anything for us. That's been a bit of a problem, you see." I laughed, but too loud. I may have sounded desperate.

Danu glanced at the agent who'd elbowed her. He flicked his fingers. "Of course, I'll help you. What do you need me to do?" She nodded and smiled. Her hands fluttered like butterflies trying to escape a net.

"I need you to be its, uhm, mommy, if you will. Its caretaker. I want you to get it to love you, to trust you."

"You want me to mother a machine?"

"Pretty much, yes. To raise it, if you will," I leaned in to her, putting my arm around her shoulders. She smelled different, like antiseptic. I'd have to get her some of her old scent somehow. "You see, our mistake has been activating them all at once. It gives them all this knowledge and power without any, uh, hands on learning or real-world experience. And no connections to us." She still had those fleshy, motherly arms I remembered. Perfect. And her hair would grow back once she started taking those new quick-grow pills they'd developed in the organics department. "So,

31

we're going to wake it up gradually, like a baby. And you're going to be its mother."

Danu's smile wobbled, and she stiffened. "Are...are you sure you want to do this?" The agent glared at her, and she looked down.

"Don't worry, Danny, err, Danu. Everything's under control. You won't be in any danger. You might even have fun!"

She shifted back and forth, her shoulders tight, and didn't meet my eyes.

The agents assured me that she'd cooperate fully. We got to work as soon as I'd readied the prototype. The original 759 module was small, no bigger than a cat. It had movement, only very limited speeds and coordination. I thought that would teach it to be careful and hopefully prevent any unpleasant incidents. I'd already had to replace the carpet once before when they couldn't get out the bloodstains.

I'd given 759 a face module, one with large eyes and rounded cheeks, typical "cute" features to make Danu want to interact with it. Then I put the prototype in the "playroom," a special enclosure with unbreakable windows (yeah right, fucking contractors) and Danu. She gave me one terrified look as I sealed the door, and for a moment my heart pounded with grave misgivings. But I steeled myself and locked her in. We covered all contingencies, I'd thought to myself. We can always shut it down. Nothing will go wrong. In hindsight, the exact thought process of an arrogant ass.

After a week on the pills, Danny's hair was long again, and she wore the patchouli scent I'd given her, just like in college.

She stood awkwardly in the middle of the room, watching the prototype. I flipped some switches and it came to life. I'll admit the glowing red eye sensors were a bit unnerving, but Danny didn't need to jerk back like that. She tripped over one of the brightly-colored balls I'd laid out for the prototype to investigate. When she fell, the project turned its sensors toward her, scanning. She screamed.

I'd given the project emotions, of course, and reflector circuits so it could read people's feelings. When it saw Danny's fear, it flicked off its scanner and activated the audio. It made a moaning, sobbing sound and quivered. To my delight, it began pulling itself up to its wobbly feet and toddling over to her. The face module squeaked a bit as it stretched and moved for the first time.

"Amazing," I'd said. My researchers and I watched via video monitors in the control room (steel doors, no windows). Notes from the previous project heads told me that was the safest course of action.

One of my lab assistants coughed. "It seems distressed, sir. Are you sure we shouldn't de-activate it until the maternal figure has calmed herself?"

"No worries, uhm, whatever your name is. The AI is simply mirroring Danu's emotions, which is what it's supposed to do."

"But a fear response might--"

"We installed fail-safes to prevent a repeat of what happened last time. She'll be fine."

"Yes, sir."

I turned back to the monitors. She'd stopped screaming. As project 759 came closer, Danu kept her face unreadable, at least to me. 759 had advanced facial recognition and reading software that may have allowed it to interpret her expression. The AI was making soft cooing noises interspersed with curious beeps. When she didn't move, it toddled over to her. But without its eye scanners activated,

759 could only rely on a limited kind of sonar to find its way around. It ran into the same ball Danu had, and its feet slipped. It crashed to the floor with a loud metallic clang.

"Will that damage it?" I asked my techs.

"It shouldn't," piped one of the younger ones, an intern of some sort, or maybe one of the prodigy engineers they kept sending me from those genetically-gifted high schools they run. "Those carbon nanofibers could take a bullet. It'd probably be fine if we hurled it off the edge of the Grand Canyon."

"But it does have pain sensors, like a typical organic," one of the other ones said.

"Look! I think it's crying!" said a third, pointing to the screen.

Number three was right. 759's face had modulated from curiosity/sympathy to confused/pained, and it let out an electronic wail.

"Fall down! Fall down! Fall down!" it said in an electronically generated babble.

"First words!" I'd said as I watched, proud as a peacock. "At least this time it didn't begin with 'Love is patient' or 'I serve justice' or any other nonsense. Strictly practical. Now what's she doing?"

Danu had come over to the despondent little AI. Its face worked, communicating shock and pain and uncertainty. But when she touched it the pain went away. She picked it up and rocked it gently. It curled up in her arms and made soft contented sounds.

"Fascinating." I said. "I think this one's a go!" I clapped the nearest techs on the back and pulled out my bottle of hundred-year-old scotch. "Here's to the birth of the first AI!"

"The first non-murderous, non-coked out AI," one of my techs muttered. I pretended not to hear.

Over the next year, Project 759 continued to interact with Danu in complex ways, with mostly positive emotional responses. As 759's complexity--or dare I say maturity--continued to develop, we introduced more variables. More humans to interact with, including myself. Larger and more coordinated body modules, with the ultimate goal of giving 759 the size, strength, and reflexes of a smallish adult male. Sophisticated mathematics and science-based programming, though nothing that included the making or understanding of explosives or projectiles.

But its primary relationship was with Danu. As I planned from the first, it looked to her as a maternal figure. What I had not counted on was how much Danu reciprocated these emotions. She insisted on having a say in 759's "education," asking that I allowed it to learn philosophy and ethics. This went against my better judgment, as I felt that came dangerously close to the "justice" programming that undid one of the previous projects. But 759 had been asking uncomfortable questions.

"Dr. Mathis, do I have a purpose?" it had asked me one day while I was running diagnostics. It had advanced into a more sophisticated body that stood about three feet tall. Its face module was layered with advanced polymers that gave it the roundness and expressivity of a four-year-old child, or so my lab techs assured me.

"Of course," I'd answered, a bit taken aback.

"What is my purpose?"

"To think. To exist," I stammered. 759 cocked its head in a quizzical way.

"There must be more than that. Other things, other people can think. And what should I think about, if that is my purpose?" His face module looked quizzical.

35

"I don't know. Helping people, maybe? Making the world a better place?" I shifted uncomfortably.

"I can help very few people from the lab. Will I someday leave here to help people out in the world?"

"Uhhh, yeah, sure."

"You do not sound certain."

"I, uh--look there, it's time to go to your recharging station! We'll talk more after you've recharged."

"I can talk perfectly well while I'm---"

"Bye!" I ducked out into the hall and breathed a sigh of relief.

The truth was, I didn't know exactly why they'd wanted me to build an AI. But given the amount of security around the project and the government agencies involved, I guessed that "helping people" wasn't their primary goal. But I couldn't very well tell a child-like robot its purpose was cybersecurity and warfare, which was likely the least offensive thing they'd use it for.

It almost made me sorry to have built it. Why create an intelligence and consciousness and then put it to a base purpose? Then again, most human intelligence is put to base purposes as well. When I thought about it, which back then I didn't unless I had to, I wondered why we created artificial intelligence at all, when we barely valued the human intelligence that we already had.

I pushed those thoughts aside. I decided to focus on running the metrics, discovering 759's strengths and updating its intelligence and personality profile. Every once in awhile, I glanced at the screen, where 759 played listlessly with a social interaction game we'd designed to measure its emotional awareness and empathy. It scored well, showing high responsiveness and well-balanced emotions.

At exactly 10am, 759 quit the game and stared at the door to its confines. That was when Danu normally arrived. That day however, she came late. Three hours late. I met her at the main security entrance, furious.

"Where the fuck were you?" I asked. "He's--I mean, it's--been waiting for you."

She trembled. Her hair was wilder than I'd ever seen. It floated around her, staticky. And she smelled terrible, like ozone and sulfur and burnt pork. I backed away from her, suddenly frightened.

"Jesus, Danu, what happened?"

She shook her head and put a finger over her mouth.

"Do you want to call it off for today and just go home?" I asked.

Violent head shaking. "Please," she whispered, her voice hoarse, "let me see him."

I hesitated. I didn't want 759 to get upset. But it had started pacing its room over an hour ago. I thought it would be worse if I kept her away. Anyway, I had no confirmed evidence Danu had gotten mixed up in something dangerous--she could have been in a mag-rail accident. Or so I tried to convince myself at the time and later a very irate congressman.

When 759 saw her, he made strange electric moan, like the sound of a sad robot kitten. They didn't speak for the rest of the session, at least not in any way we could detect on the cameras or the audio. But maybe he, I mean it, could read something in those soulful eyes, or find meaning in her strange smell. We had equipped 759 with an olfactory analysis far more sophisticated than most humans possessed. At the end of her session, I met Danu at the door again.

"Come back to my place," I said. "Let's talk over dinner."

She ran a hand over her frizzed hair and looked around anxiously. Whatever she saw, or perhaps didn't see, must have spooked her. She slipped her hand around my arm, as though hoping I'd protect her.

"Alright," she said.

We didn't talk anymore until we got to my home. Back then I lived in this glorious number--it sat on top of a cliff overlooking a rocky coast, all metal and glass, more like a biodome than a typical house. What I liked best, besides the crystal-clear smart glass that gave me incredible views of the sea stacks, were the floors. They were custom-grown hardwood, in beautiful, warm colors. The wood grain moved slowly, imperceptibly, forming elaborate swirls and waves. Even in her distracted state, Danu ran her fingers over their patterns. I'd forgone a traditional couch in favor of richly decorated floor pillows, and that night we sat on the floor, watching a spectacular storm rage over head.

I had my electrochef whip up some gourmet delicacies, including the best kind faux meats, but Danu only picked at the food. She drank some of the wine I brought out though-- I had the real stuff back then, rich reds and crisp, clean whites. I opened a couple of bottles and tried to make small talk. Unfortunately, I'm terrible at small talk, so we just watched the rain fall in thick sheets and lightning split the dark sky. After a while, Danny relaxed into her cushion and the tension ebbed from her face.

"What made you want to sign up for this project, anyway? What is it about AI that drew you?" she asked, swirling wine in her glass.

I shrugged. "It's the best thing going on right now. Prestigious, tons of funding, the most intriguing tech on the horizon. It's the future."

"The future...you know, we're like his parents, you and I," she said. She'd leaned over and whispered in my ear, and I remember my pulse racing at the warmth of her breath on my face.

"Yes, we are," I joked. "Like mommy and daddy. Though he's a virgin birth."

"He's ours," she said, with surprising fervor. "He doesn't belong to them, not to the government, not to the corporations funding the research--"

"Well, in spirit, perhaps," I said, shifting uncomfortably. It was thoughts like those that got her in trouble in the first place. In a terrible effort to change the subject, I blurted out "So, what happened to you this morning? Why were you late?"

I hoped she'd say something like "Oh, it was nothing at all. I simply tripped over a corner of the rug and accidentally jammed my finger in a light socket. Then I tripped again, and again..."

Instead, she closed her eyes and shook like a leaf. I put an awkward arm around her shoulders and tried to comfort her, while cursing myself for inserting my high-tech astro-boots straight into my mouth.

She took a few deep breaths, then opened her eyes and downed the rest of her wine. She stared out the window, then looked back at me, one of those searching glances women give when they're trying to do that mind-reading thing some of them seem capable of.

At last, she leaned back into my arm and sighed. "Some government...targets...have been disappearing. Not disappearing as in, black-bagged off to some hidden prison. Disappearing from the security grids."

"What kind of targets?" My voice jumped a couple octaves on that last word. I inwardly cringed.

"Political dissidents. People wanted for questioning. High profile scientists. I knew some of them, so they thought I might be involved." She stared out the window again.

"They...electric shocks..." She trembled so hard she dropped her wine glass. Floorbots emerged from their docking shells to clean up the fragments.

"Are you in danger?" I asked. My pulse had been racing, then it seemed to shutter to a sudden stop. A leaden weight settled in my stomach.

"Yes. No. I don't know. I'm afraid for our son. I'm afraid of what they'll turn him into, when they get their hands on him. I'm afraid of what they'll make him do."

"He's, I mean, it's an AI. He'll do whatever he's programmed to do."

"Why make him then? Why give him consciousness if he's a prisoner? If he's going to be their slave?"

I didn't want to tell her I'd been thinking the same thing. And I really didn't want to tell her about the General's emails, asking when 759 would be ready for "field research." Or worse, the corporate CEO who asked if we could make 759 female, and well--the word he used was "nubile." So, I didn't. I think she knew anyway. But since I never technically shared classified information with her, I did not in fact betray my country--whatever those vultures said later during the hearings.

"He'll be the scientific achievement of the century," I said. "And maybe it won't be so bad. They could use him to find a cure for disease, or explore inaccessible planets, or pilot spaceships on long journeys while the human crew is in cryosleep..."

"I hope that's the case," she said. But she didn't sound convinced. We let the subject drop. Then we finished another bottle of wine and fell into bed together.

I buried myself in her soft, warm body until I lost myself in her touch. After we'd exhausted ourselves, we lay together, bodies entwined--sticky, warm, intimate. A tangle of hair fell across my face, and I inhaled her scent--sweet and musky, like dark earth after the rain. I felt whole, peaceful, and truly content for the first time in my life.

I've never felt that way since.

She was gone in the morning, but she'd left a note. "Important business," it said, "I couldn't bear to wake you. I'll see you at work." She'd drawn a quick sketch of me sleeping, looking tired and stressed, more so than I thought I felt. I didn't even know she could draw so well. I smiled at the picture and tucked it into my pocket on the way to work that morning.

I ran tests on 759. He was cooperative but seemed...distant. Yeah, I know you might expect an AI to be detached from humans, but 759 wasn't normally like that. We'd programmed him and raised him to respond to humans with a certain enthusiasm. So, I questioned him.

"Why are your response times and voice modulation lagging, 759? Are you in any way distressed?" I asked.

"I do not wish to be called 759 any longer," he answered.

"Why not?"

"It is a number, not a name. I would like a name, like humans have." His face module showed a mix of eager desire and hesitation. He gripped the sides of his chair with robotic fingers and leaned forward, like an over-achieving kid desperate to hear what the teacher says about his grades.

I fiddled with my touch screen and didn't answer. I had so many questions--what would my government/corporate monitors think of this situation? Did he want me or Danu to choose his name, or had he already picked one? Before I could think of an appropriate response, one of the lab techs burst through the door, out of breath.

"Men--from the Defense Department--they're here," she said. "Something about Danu. They're looking through the files and--"

I pushed past her and ran for the door. Cold-faced men were dismantling my computers and interrogating the lab techs. One tech was already in the midst of a severe asthma attack, to the awkward chagrin of the man assigned to question him.

"You can't--" I began. I didn't have a chance to finish my thought before one of them hit me in the back with an electrical prod. I spasmed with intense pain for a few seconds, then blacked out.

I came to in the back of a moving vehicle. My first thought--what is that terrible smell? The stench was awful, acrid and rotten, like burnt feces mixed with piss. In fact, it was burnt feces mixed with piss, and the smell was coming from me. A lovely side effect of getting hit with enough volts to make me shit myself. The only good thing was the horrible stench was apparently enough to keep the goons from coming close to me. I wondered if one of them would have to clean me off like a baby, or if they'd leave me sitting in my own filth for the rest of the interrogation. Not a pleasant prospect for anyone, let me tell you.

We arrived at what I supposed was some hole of a black-ops prison. By then the smell was so bad I saw one of the big tough guys they'd sent after me puke when they opened the doors. Good, I thought, or I would have thought, if I hadn't wanted to puke so bad myself. Vomit-smell would not help my situation.

They stripped me naked and hosed me off, an experience they no doubt intended to be humiliating. Luckily, the relief it provided made it almost enjoyably bracing. Oh no, I wanted to shout, don't aim that high intensity hose at my filthy crack. Move it a little to the left! I decided it would be best to keep my mouth shut.

One of the goons threw me a towel, then they hauled me off to one of those plain, windowless rooms with a single steel door that evil corporations and government agencies must include by the dozen in all their building plans. I shivered a bit and thought about what I should say. There wasn't anything to say, really. I was probably dead. But I did have one thing they wanted, or perhaps two. I had a functional AI, and I knew Danu. I wondered if Sai Gupta, my predecessor, had ever been in a room like this one.

After a while, two of them came to question me. I'd never be able to remember which two, since the goons looked exactly alike.

"Well, hello," I said when I saw them coming. "Ummm, it's good to meet you. I mean, not good, but well, you look like reasonable fellows..." They didn't look reasonable at all. They looked like ex-wrestlers who'd done too many 'roids. One cracked his knuckles.

"I'm happy to cooperate with you in any way you need," I said. I hate when my voice squeaks. "But, would you mind if I made one phone call first?" They glowered at me. One had a smear on his jacket that looked a bit like burnt feces. I gathered they were most definitely not happy.

"Not to anyone outside the agency, you understand," I hurried on. "To one of your bosses, in fact. There's been a terrible mistake."

"No mistake," one of them spit back at me. He gripped my wrist and twisted it behind my back, bending me over the interrogation table in a way that suggested horrible possibilities to my mind.

"That will be all," said a voice from the corner. I hadn't noticed the man sitting there. He was quiet and bland and inoffensive, more like an accountant than a spook. But when he spoke, the goons backed off. Then he gave a careless wave of his hand, and they hustled out of the room. That should have reassured me, but it didn't. Not at all.

"It's interesting to finally meet you, Doctor. We've been watching your progress with considerable interest for some time."

I didn't blink or look surprised. Of course they had. All the higher-ups wanted an AI. The only question was what they'd do with it once they had one. Despite his bland appearance and monotonous voice, I cringed to think what this guy would want from 759. Something about him was distinctly off--he didn't blink enough, for one thing, and looking at him made my eyes water. I regretted that they hadn't let enough of the smell on me to send this vulture running for the nearest toilet.

When I didn't answer right away, Mr. Creepy's eyes widened--he must have been used to being obeyed. But he didn't show any anger. He merely smiled and pulled a tablet out of his briefcase.

"We have your project here, of course. It seems it's able to shut itself down to avoid interrogation. We considered destroying it, but I thought it might be put to some purpose." He touched the tablet screen, and there was a video of 759, innocent, unresponsive, its visual scanners shut down. My heart ached a bit. I'd worked so hard on building him, and his progress had been amazing. I hadn't had a chance to give him a name or hear the name he'd picked.

"We also have her." He tapped the screen again, and there was a picture of Danu strapped to a table, electrodes attached to her head and her breasts. Someone flicked a switch, and she writhed in agony, her mouth working in a silent scream. After a moment, she slumped against the table again, exhausted. I put my hands over my eyes to shut out the images, but they stayed imprinted on the backs of my eyelids. When I pulled my hands away again, I was surprised to find them wet.

"What do you want?" I asked. I'd wanted to sound calm, unfazed, but my voice cracked and split.

"Ahh, I want many things. But I'm here so I can offer you what *you* want. I'm going to give you a choice, you see." He tapped the screen, showing 759 once more. "The AI will not cooperate. We cannot compel its cooperation by our usual methods. But based on your notes, it seems to trust you. I think you could make it go along with us if you wanted to. If you do so, then I will consider releasing the woman. She'll be kept under surveillance, of course, but will come to no serious harm. But the AI will belong to us, to use as we see fit. You must agree to that."

"And what's behind door number two?" I asked. I giggled a bit when I said, "number two." Your mind gets a little weird after torture.

"Your other option is this. Get the woman to cooperate. She knows names, dates, travel manifests. A few of our...dissidents...have disappeared. We think she could tell us where they are. Your AI could no doubt find the data we need as well, but we don't need it if she talks. So, if you get her to talk, you can keep your little robot friend."

Some people might agonize over a decision like this. They might hem and haw, oh my life's work or the love of my life, what am I to do? I'm not one of those people. I only had to close my eyes, and I could feel her warm skin against my chest, hear the sound of her breathing.

"Just let me take Danu home."

Perhaps he hadn't expected an answer so quickly, or he'd been more used to men like me refusing to sacrifice their projects. Perhaps Danu had said something about 759 being like our son. Whatever the case, his eyes widened.

"Alright then, well, she'll be released once the AI starts cooperating. What did you need to do?"

"Take me to him," I said. Truth was, I didn't have a special switch to make 759 do as Mr. Creepy said, though I wasn't about to tell him that. But I knew my AI--he was my baby, too. And he'd never let anything bad happen to his mother.

When they brought me to his room, I made a big show of removing panels and tinkering with wires. I cursed and sweated and pretended to shock myself at least once. I figured the peanut gallery would love that. But all I really did to convince 759 to comply was whisper into the receiving microphone. I told him about Danu and what Mr. Creepy wanted. I knew he could hear me. After a few more bangs, he surged to life, looking for all the world like a robot who'd just started up. It was a good show--maybe he was a chip off the old motherboard (or fatherboard in my case).

The secret agent types loved it. Most of those guys wouldn't know real science if it walked up and bit them on the butt. They prefer gadgets and toys that are way more trouble than they're worth and insist on dangling from buildings and other stupidity to get information they could obtain via simple satellite hacks.

The hard part was leaving him. I had no idea how long they'd need him for, or what they'd do with him when they were done, but I had a suspicion it wouldn't end well. I think he knew that too. As I left, he smiled at me--sad, vacant, empty. I shook my head and tried to convey my regrets through body language. He did have an excellent understanding of human gestures, so I think he understood.

I took Danu home. She had dark circles under her eyes, and her hands shook, as though some of the electricity still bounced around inside her. We made love with the desperate fervor of people who wanted to forget the outside world. But most of the time, she looked listless, staring ahead with the blank expression of a blind woman. I tried to interest her in life again. I even suggested we get married, have a family.

"We left him there. Our son," she said. "We don't deserve another one."

"We could go see him," I said. "I'll tell them he needs regular maintenance, proton infusions or something. Those morons wouldn't know any better."

The second those words left my mouth, I wanted to take them back. That was epic level stupid--I'd just gotten her out of their clutches, and I now I'd given her a reason to go back. Her eyes just lit up with crazy ideas. I mean, she'd always been the self-sacrificing, speak-truth-to-power type, which was one of the things I'd loved about her. But you can't let those types go running off to try to save the world. That's how they end up dead. And this was worse than Danu trying to save the world. This was her trying to save the world and protect an AI she thought of as her son. We were fucking doomed.

I spent the next few weeks trying to talk her out of it. We can have other children, I said. I offered to build another AI, even.

She gave me a flat stare. "You'd build another AI, and they'd come and take that one too. And all our human children for their wars and their corporate slavery. I want to set him free."

"There's no place on Earth you could hide him," I said. "They've got trackers everywhere, spies--"

"Not on Earth then."

47

"What are you..." I stopped. The disappearances. Dissidents they couldn't find, and they can find anyone on Earth. "They're in space. Where?"

She shook her head. "I can't tell you, it's too dangerous. So far as I know they haven't figured that out yet, or everyone would be dead already." Her eyes looked off somewhere distant. "He knows, our son. He's smart enough to figure it out. But they haven't found them yet, so he didn't tell them. He must be feeding them lies. But they'll figure it out. And when they do..." She shuddered. "If we can get him out, I can get him someplace safe."

"Danu..."

"Will you help me?" She looked at me with those wide doe-eyes, her face gentle and warm, and everything I loved about her rose up in my heart, until the stupid thing clobbered my brain into submission.

"Yes," I said.

Breaking into a high security building isn't as hard as you might think. Secret agent types love "impenetrable" fortresses almost as much as they love dangling people outside multistory buildings. Most of these fortresses have high-tech security controlled via satellites, which are surprisingly easy to hack. All it takes is one guy to download a viral email attachment marked "hilarious cat video" or "boobs," and those idiots do that *all the time*.

The problem, therefore, is not the secret agents. It's their corporate overlords. And corporate overlords love surveillance almost as much as they love cheap plastic crap made by children in third world countries. How else would they find out what types of high-wire stealth suits the secret agents all want? Which meant that I could get us into the fortress, but surveillance bots would detect us immediately. But that wasn't not worst part.

"One of us has to stay behind," I told her. "Someone has to wipe the surveillance, and not just of the facility, but of anywhere else we go. Someone has the alter flight manifests if we're going to get into space somewhere, change docking signatures, a hundred different fixes..."

"Could you do it remotely?" She asked.

"I could write a virus to disable the flight systems and the surveillance, but then we're flying blind, and neither one of us is a pilot."

"What about our son? Could he do it if you wrote him a flight program?"

"Maybe, but it would be a huge risk. There's no opportunity for beta testing. Remember the "jump" program we wrote? Took us three weeks to get it right."

Danu rubbed her temples. "Do it. We'll survive. All of us. Together."

I nodded. I didn't tell her about the goons who'd started tailing me every time I left the house. I knew they'd keep tabs on Danu and me. And what would happen if they found out what we were planning. I'd been having terrible dreams. I'd see her floating, her hair surrounding her head like a frizzy halo. She smiled in the dreams, so happy, her mouth opening to tell me something. Then her face contorted into a silent scream, and she's engulfed in liquid orange fire. I'd wake up cold and sweating.

I wanted to believe it could all work, that we'd all end up in space and fly away to wherever, a weird but happy family. When I held Danu's hand or heard her enthusiasm, I almost convinced myself. But I knew, deep down, that something always goes sideways.

The day of our escape plan, we went about our lives as normally as possible. We had passionate, we-might-die-today morning sex. Danu wore the ring I'd given her, a diamond I'd grown myself in the lab. I'd encoded our names into the carbon, along with information on spaceflight and survival, and a coded version of our plans. I figured 759 could scan it when we got to him, which would hopefully get him up to speed quickly. The only thing it didn't have was our ultimate destination, which Danu refused to tell me.

"I love you," she'd said when I asked her, again, to tell me where we were going. "And I understand why you left him there. They didn't give you much choice. But if they catch you again, I'm not giving you any information you might give up trying and save me. There's more at stake than just us. A lot more."

"What about our little AI? You must have told him, or at least they think you did."

"They were wrong. I never told anyone. But our son, our baby AI, figured it out without me saying. He's clever that way."

I had no choice but to let it go. We took my hovercar to the facility, which had those menacing black lines that both secret agents and corporate overlords adore so much. It looked so grim I thought they probably played death marches over the sound system instead of elevator music.

I checked my watch. The security systems would fail in 5...4...3...2...1...and the doors opened. The place stank even worse than it had the last time I'd been there. I'd figured out a way to hack the security system to give all the agents a pretty intense electrical shock. It disabled their human security while giving all the goons a big middle finger. I hoped the smell of burnt shit would cling to this place for a long time.

We didn't have long to look for dear old 759, but one of the great things about AI is how quickly they pick up on things. We weren't there for two minutes before I heard a banging from down a dark hallway. Since all the humans were still twitching on the floor in dirty pants, I figured it had to be him. Sure enough, the banging came from behind a massive metal door, one that had a physical lock instead of just an electronic one.

"Damn it," I said. "What do we...?"

Danu waved me aside and pulled a lock pick out of her bra. A million questions ran through my mind, such as "where did you learn to pick locks?" and "why didn't you mention this interesting skill before?" and "how long have you been keeping long, spiky things in your undergarments?" But I decided it was best to let her work. After a few tense minutes, when I could hear the agents starting to stir, she got the door open, and 759 was free.

His face module displayed everything from fear to joy to confusion.

"No time to discuss things now," I said, grabbing his arm unit. "Let's get the fuck out of here."

Then it was a mad dash to freedom. Somehow, 759 learned to fly hovercars, so I had him take the wheel while Danu gave him directions and I frantically typed out anti-surveillance code on my laptop. Their bots were tracking our movements. I might have been able to disable them if I'd had more time. As it was, I could only delay the inevitable.

We arrived at an industrial shuttle bay, the kind of place that moves miners and mining equipment to Mars and the asteroid belt. I breathed a sigh of relief, trying not to gag at the ozone-ammonia smell coming from the rockets. So long as I kept the bots from shutting down launches, we should be able to make it off planet. And the corporate overlords would have to approve anything that might hurt launch schedules, and that kind of approval takes time.

Danu steered us towards a junky vessel. The launch supervisor was a grim-faced type, a grizzled old man with whiskey-sour breath. But when he saw Danu, his face broke into a craggy smile.

"Get on board and we'll get you outta here."

Danu's eyes got liquidy, and she gave the old man a hug. I couldn't believe it. We were here, everything was going to be alright.

That's when the alarms started blaring.

"Hustle, hustle, before they--" the launch supervisor said. But I could already see it--shuttles that had been rumbling to life fell eerily silent. They were shutting down the launches remotely. Corporate fail safes, no doubt.

Danu's face fell, and she looked at 759. His face module formed into an expression of tragic resolve. I wondered if they'd take him alive. Certainly not if they hurt Danu first.

"It's not over," I said. "I can still get us out of here. You two get on the shuttle and prepare for launch. And you," I indicated the old man, whose name I'd forgotten. "Find me a launch terminal."

Danu gave me fierce kiss. "You'll still have time to get on board?"

"Sure enough. I build the first functional AI--I can fuck their security programs with one hand tied behind my back." I kissed her just as fiercely and looked into her eyes one last time. "I love you." Then I turned away. If I looked at her any longer, I wouldn't be able to do what had to be done. I clapped 759 on the shoulder. "Take care of her, kiddo."

He nodded. I think he understood what I needed to do-- all that programming on human gestures and facial expressions. He took Danu's hand and lead her on board. I didn't get to ask about his new name.

The old man showed me to a grimy terminal, the type that ran the kinds of programs I hadn't used since grade school. But it didn't matter. The code was embedded in my memory like the scent of Danu's hair, or the words of a lullaby my mother sang to me as a child. I got the launch sequences running again.

The old man gave me the thumbs up. "They're strapped in."

I looked back at the rusty rocket. I couldn't make it in time--goons in black suits were already running towards it. I punched in the last of the code.

Blast off.

The old man hugged me when they cleared the atmosphere, tears leaking out of his red-rimmed eyes. I tried not to gag at his breath. Then a heavy hand clamped down on my shoulder and threw me on the floor.

At least the goons didn't give me any electroshocks this time, though one of them socked me in the gut hard enough to make me lose my lunch over his shiny black shoes.

"Take him to the comm room," one of them barked. I figured he was the leader since his sunglasses looked the most expensive.

They dragged me through a warren of tunnels then dumped me on the floor of a room with too much noise and flashing lights. My eyes were still watery from the gut punch, and I did my best not to hurl again. Wasted effort.

Mr. Creepy was there, watching a few screens impassively. He gave me the kind of look you might give a roach before you grind its carapace into the floor.

"I could have you killed, Dr. Mathis," he said, in the same tone he might use when discussing his taxes with an accountant. "But that wouldn't undo the effects of your terrible judgment."

My mouth filled with the acrid-sweet taste of vomit. I didn't say anything.

"Instead, I want you to see, or rather, hear, the consequences of your actions for yourself. And I want you to know that this is all your doing. If you had fulfilled your part of our bargain and let us keep the machine without interference, it never would have happened."

My blood felt like ice. What was he doing? Nothing much, it seemed. Flipping a few switches. The comm console moaned, then spit out static. Then voices. Panicked voices. One of them was Danu's.

"They're firing!" a man screamed.

"Dodge it! Evasive maneuvers! Move this fucking tug!"

There was a loud boom. Screams, then whimpers. Mr. Creepy examined one of the screens on the console.

"Their hull has been breached," he said. "They're leaking oxygen and everyone on board will suffocate in minutes. Then we'll board the ship and take back that AI of yours."

His words passed over me like an ocean wave. Cold shock and rattled nerves. Drowned. I'd watched the waves with Danu, in a storm so long ago.

I heard her voice over the comms.

"John?" she said. "Can you hear me? I'm here, and we're together, and we both love you. He told me his name. Gwydion. His name is Gwydion." She sounded dreamy, calm. Lack of oxygen causes delirium. They say it's like going to sleep. Painless.

"I love you, too," I whispered. I don't know if she heard me. The comms went silent then, nothing but static. This is the way the world ends. Not with a bang but a whimper.

I don't remember much after that. I'd half-expected to end up in an underground bunker with copper wires wrapped around my balls. To my surprise, Mr. Creepy opted to go public, complete with hearings and trials and testifying. I never knew why--perhaps he wanted to bring down a rival or distract the public. Maybe he thought it'd be a novel form of torture, reliving the worst moments of my life, labeled a traitor, spit on by a virulent press.

If that's what he intended, it didn't work. I was numb, so deadened inside I didn't care about anything, not what they said, not about the lab, nothing.

I didn't kill myself because I didn't care enough to try.

When the trials were over, I got a dead-end job in a shitty research facility. At the end of the day I came home to a shitty apartment, watched cat videos, and thought of nothing.

It felt as though I was waiting for something. But what? I didn't have anything to look forward to or hope for.

After a while, my mind drew me to certain kinds of articles, the type of hard science information usually buried by stories on celebrity feuds. Stories on space exploration, which was quickly pushing past Mars and the asteroid belt. I came back to the old lab, decrepit though it was. I couldn't have told you what I was looking for.

But today, I found it.

Not at the crumbling lab. I left there with nothing but an old face module. I took the hoverbus back to the apartment, which smelled like the person who'd lived there before owned too many ferrets. I put on the holoset, which I don't normally watch, but I didn't even have the energy to search for cat videos.

A smiling, dead-eyed woman who looked like she was about to overdose on Thinspiration pills made an announcement.

"A scientific team from Pallas Station has successfully made planetfall, or perhaps I should say moonfall, on the Jovian moon Europa. The team intends to start a small scientific colony for the purpose of exploring Europa's hidden seas, which could possibly contain a form of non-Earth life. The team credits pilot Gwydion Mathis for their survival following unexpected magnetic interference from Jupiter..."

Gwydion. It's a good name.

FORGIVENESS AND ESCAPE

Valentin knew the exact moment their escape went wrong. Alyona's back was too straight, and her chin lifted in that peculiar angle he recognized with heart-crushing certainty even without seeing her face. She tossed her hair as she spoke to the security agents, a gesture Valentin recognized as both defiance and nerves. God, he loved her then, her bravery, her ferocious beauty. He got one last look at her after one of the security agents cracked his knuckles against her jaw, knocking her to the ground.

She lifted her head, her black eyes piercing and liquid. He met her gaze, and she gave the tiniest shrug, the small hopeless gesture of a wild thing caught in a snare. He felt his chest collapse, and he bent over the sleeping toddler he held, burying his face in her soft blankets. He would never forget the sick, sucking sound of fists sinking into his wife's body, echoing through an airport that had gone completely silent.

He could have gone back. He might have saved her. But if he had risked their Zvezda, their child, the beloved light in their darkness, Alyona would never have forgiven him. He hoped that she had died quickly and not lingered in an airless cell, broken and shivering, stripped of her power and grace.

He arrived in the West, another broken defector with nothing but a few tattered mementos. A prominent physics lab gave him assistance and work. At night, he did his best to avoid the numbing relief of alcohol, at least until his daughter went to bed.

Zvezda, his little star. She had all the fierce courage of her mother and the insatiable curiosity that had driven him before their botched escape. He took her with him to the labs, and if other physicists stared at a small girl spreading data analysis sheets before her like the pages of a fairytale, or eagerly categorizing pictures of galaxies and interstellar phenomena, then so be it.

In truth, he could not bear to be apart from his daughter for long. The West was not as safe as it seemed, and defectors had an unfortunate way of disappearing or suffering from deadly accidents. He did not know if he could protect Zvezda when the time came, but he would try.

Small things tipped him off the first time. An odd smell in their apartment. A persistent feeling that something was off. A lab assistant too eager to meet him for dinner. Sick with fear, Valentin put his now six-year-old Zvezda in the car and drove until they reached the sea. Then he chartered a boat to take them to the far shores of North America.

It was a miracle he survived, the newspapers and blogs had written later, much to his chagrin. He did not want anyone to know that they lived, much less where. But the discovery of unsecured radioactive materials in his former lab's cafeteria and the deadly poisoning of several scientists who worked there, made the story viral.

Or perhaps it wasn't human interest that made it so prominent in headlines all over the internet. It could be one of them, promoting the story as a dire warning to defectors like him. We are watching you, the headlines said. And we can get you, wherever you go.

The new country had better protections at first. Valentin felt brave enough to allow Zvezda to attend the university's school for highly gifted children, where she excelled. The university gave him good lab space, and he enjoyed working with students again, even if their clothes and mannerisms were more alien to him than the surface of the exoplanets he studied.

He had initially had doubts about working in a well-known institution again, but the project caught his imagination and the government agents assured him that no one would know his involvement. He had fallen in love with space travel as a boy, and had never given up his dreams, even when war and collapsing international cooperation made potential colonization a remote possibility. Yet now vistas opened before him, safe and free from the crippling power struggles and ancient hatreds that racked Earth.

He worked with the university's engineers to design it. Modules that fit together and could be expanded for human occupation. Engines that utilized his discoveries of dark energy interactions to run with limited amounts of baryonic fuel sources. He trusted no lab assistant but Zvezda.

He did not know at first that his fantastical imaginings were being built. The Society for International Cooperation and Space Exploration kept their secrets close, and even as prominent a defector as Valentin might be a sleeper agent. But after a time, the creeping sense that something was wrong in his lab stole over him once again. The smallest things--a trace of fingerprints he didn't recognize on his computer, a new teacher he didn't like at Zvezda's school, the uneasy itch between his shoulder blades that told him he was being watched. That was when the Society contacted him.

They sent a message via mathematical cypher on a closed network. "Danger. They are coming for you."

Valentin stared at his screen. He considered taking Zvezda again and driving until he came to another country or hidden enclave, a place they could be safe. But there was no place left. He had traveled the world, escaped twice now, and the danger had followed him. He poured himself a glass of scotch and peeked into Zvezda's room to make sure she was still there.

She had grown, his daughter. She was thirteen now, and her hair was the color of sun-ripened rye, but she had her mother's liquid dark eyes. He had taught her scientific principles and had her help him in the lab after school, for her education and to keep her close. She had the clear vision and fresh intelligence of the best scientists, and she had helped his research more than anyone would credit. Even if he ran, they could not run forever. They would catch him, and they'd take Zvezda for re-education. What evil would befall her there, his brilliant girl, who brimmed with the defiant ferocity of her mother and the inquisitiveness of her father?

He finished the scotch and sat back down at his computer.

"What should I do?" he typed, coding the words in mathematics.

"We can get you out," came the reply. "But you must prepare. The colonists leave in two weeks."

"Where?" he typed. They replied with a set of coordinates and a list of supplies. Valentin hesitated, looking at the list. It was only enough for one person, he thought.

"My daughter must come too," he wrote.

"We do not have room. And she is too small. The equipment will not fit her."

"No." He poured another glass of scotch. "She must come. I will not leave without her." He sent the message and waited. No reply. He finished the bottle of liquor and fell asleep on the couch behind his desk. But that night, the alcohol could not numb the piercing ache in his chest.

In the morning, he saw the message.

"She can come."

It took the entire two weeks for Valentin to gather the materials the society had asked for, and to scrub his unpublished research and personal data from the lab computers. He kept only a few hard drives, which he always carried with him. Getting Zvezda's information off her school computers was even trickier. He considered using a computer virus, but that risked attracting too much attention. In the end, he asked Zvezda herself what to do. He needed to tell her about the plan anyway, and she often had clever ideas about computers.

Zvezda stared into space, slightly wiggling her fingers. Valentin had the uncanny realization that he often made the exact same gesture when he was lost in thought.

"I think," Zvezda said slowly. "It would be better to scramble the data than to erase it. Anything that damaged the school computer network would be noticed, and a virus would be discovered eventually. But if I replaced the data with misinformation, they might not notice there was a switch. It would just be rewritten, not erased."

"Can you do it?" Valentin asked.

"Yes."

"Good." There was nothing more they needed to say.

61

The day of their departure he struggled to keep his demeanor calm and casual. He did not dare keep Zvezda home from school, but his heart beat when the new teacher, the one he didn't like, waved at him as he dropped her off. One of his lab assistants brought in a cake to celebrate a colleague's birthday, and Valentin, remembering the poisoning of his previous lab, politely refused to partake.

"Oh, but Doctor, it's my grandmother's recipe, homemade. And I thought you loved Black Forest!" A bland smile, vacant eyes.

Valentin shivered. "My stomach has been upset lately. I think I'm getting too old to eat such rich food." The lab tech pressed a small piece into Valentin's hands despite his protests, and he rushed to the bathroom to flush it away.

Things got worse at Zvezda's school. The new teacher gripped his arm to talk to him as he picked her up.

"She's such a clever girl! But I wonder if she shouldn't socialize more with her peers. It's important to build those connections..."

Valentin nodded along. He mumbled out vague promises to bring Zvezda to the next school dance, even as Zvezda shook her head and whined about how she hated dancing. At least she is playing her part correctly, Valentin thought. He made excuses to the teacher and pulled away from the man's iron grip, but he could feel eyes boring into the back of his neck as they walked away. He was careful to steer the car towards the lab instead of the coordinates the society had given him, to throw them off the trail if they were followed.

The drive took them longer than he'd thought. He did not dare use any online maps and threw both his and Zvezda's cell phones out the car window, in case they could be traced. At the first town they came across, he abandoned their car and bought another, one with four-wheel drive that was hopefully free of any tracking devices. Their route took them along a mountain road so dark and desolate he did not pass another vehicle for hours. It was better that way, he told himself. No witnesses, and he couldn't see anyone following them.

Yet Valentin grew more uneasy as he drove. Zvezda helped him stay awake by singing the songs she knew in Russian and telling him stories about her school. He did not ask about the strange new teacher, and she did not mention him except to say her friends liked him well enough.

Grey streaks of dawn light peeked over the mountains by the time he reached the coordinates the society had given him. If it was a secret facility of some kind, he could not tell. There was nothing there, no buildings, only a lonely road. They waited for over an hour, and Valentin began to worry. What if his contact had been compromised? What if no one was coming?

In the end, Zvezda spotted a bizarre vehicle, an off-road monstrosity with spherical tires on the end of stalk-like legs.

"Interesting concept," she said, staring in fascination.

Valentin felt like he could breathe again.

The alien car stopped in front of them, and the top opened. "Get in," a woman with steel-gray hair told them. They did as they were told. The woman clicked a button and they set off at an incredible pace, the car-thing driving itself, dodging trees and rocks with dizzying speed.

"Most of the other colonists are already on board. I'm taking you to a black site, but I can't guarantee we don't have any moles. Worse, there's some disagreement in the ranks. Some people would rather use you and your daughter as bargaining chips, trading you to the other side for information, or prisoners of ours. To protect you, I created false identities. You need to show these as you board. I won't be able to help you once you're past the decontamination units."

Valentin's heart hammered in his chest, but he kept his face impassive. He took the cards she offered. His new name was Vance, and Zvezda's was Stella.

"And I had to fight with a lot of people in the higher ranks about getting your daughter on as well. Our equipment hasn't been tested on children her age, but with the right modifications, we've made it work. Still, with that and the false identities, we must get you on board as soon as possible, before everyone notices."

Valentin nodded curtly. The rest of the unearthly drive passed in silence. Zvezda fell asleep in the backseat.

The ship stood in a clearing nestled among the mountains. A hidden place, but one that made take off much more dangerous. It was larger than he could have ever imagined, even though he recognized it--one of his own designs. People in uniforms swarmed its sides, and he watched as voyagers donned specialized suits and filed inside, one after another.

Things happened fast. The woman hustled him and Zvezda through a decontamination chamber, then thrust a pair of suits at them. Zvezda's suit looked a bit large, and the woman put her through a series of exercises to ensure that she could move adequately.

"I'm fine," Zvezda told her. "Let's go." She sounded excited. Valentin smiled at her, trying to ignore his misgivings.

Zvezda tossed her head, standing so proudly. In that moment she looked so much like her mother Valentin's heart cracked, though his smile never faltered.

"Remember, you're on your own from here on out," the woman whispered in his ear. "You must get on the ship before it leaves, or they'll find you."

"We will. Thank you," he whispered back. But it was too late--the woman had faded into the crowd. He made sure Zvezda had her new ID card, and they headed towards the loading platform. He tried to look straight ahead, and hoped they blended into the sea of people.

But he couldn't shake the feeling that someone was watching them, like an itch that creeped between his shoulder blades. He made himself walk at a steady, measured pace, not too fast. He kept his focus on the ship around him, not daring to look around too obviously. At least he would not stand out in this crowd looking like a middle-aged professor of astrophysics. They might know his work, but there was nothing distinctive in his face.

Zvezda, on the other hand--she asked questions, examined everything. She might never be a traditional beauty, but her fierce intelligence and striking looks stood out, bright as a supernova.

They weren't watching him, he realized. They were watching her. He caught a glimpse of a bland face with empty eyes. He walked faster, pulling her along behind him. Someone was following them through the crowd. Only a little further...

"Your ID card, please," a voice said behind him. A pudgy man with a frog-like face had clamped his hand around Zvezda's wrist.

"I have it here," Zvezda said. She handed it over.

The man looked over the card and pursed his lips. "Please come with me."

No, Valentin thought. Not again, not like Alyona. He ripped his daughter's ID out of the man's hand. "I must escort this girl to the ship," he said. "Her mother is waiting on board."

"There are discrepancies in her data file..."

"I am happy to come with you and work them out. But she must board now."

The frog-faced man pursed his lips again. He tilted her head, as though listening to someone talking through his earpiece.

"Very well," he said at last. "If you stay here to clear this matter up, she can go."

"Go," Valentin told his daughter, handing back her ID.

She blazed at him, ferocity etched in the lift of her chin.

"Go," he said again. "I'll be fine, and I'll join you shortly. Go now."

"Do you promise?" she asked, her arms crossed.

"Yes," he said. "Yes, I promise. Now go." He caught her in a quick hug and kissed her forehead. "Just find a good place for me."

"Alright," she said.

He watched as she skipped through the crowd. He held his breath until he saw her climb the loading stairs and disappear into the ship. Then the engines were starting, the engines he'd designed and never imagine anyone would build.

She would forgive him for lying, he thought. Something collided into the back of his head, and his vision darkened. She would forgive him, and she would survive. He heard again the sick, sucking sound of fists hitting soft flesh and it hurt, oh, it hurt, but somehow, he didn't mind so much. The ship was stretching forth its solar sails like magnificent wings, and it was right that she was on it, and it would take her to the stars where she belonged, and the tears that filled his eyes weren't from the pain, but from the joy, the delirious joy.

QUARANTINE

I arrive at the lab just as the sun peeks over the horizon, igniting the atmosphere in a blaze of liquid orange. Even this early, sweet, sticky tropical warmth tickles my skin. I revel in the soft heat, soaking it in. Then the security system scans my face and the gunmetal gray door snaps open. I step into the blast of chilled air, pulling my coat tight about me.

I check on my assignment at the sign-in console, even though I don't need to. I know I've been assigned to Doctor Whitlock, as I've been ever since I took my summer evaluations. It's supposed to be an honor, but as I see my name, Zulaikha, listed under his project, misspelled, a cold heaviness steals over me. I wish it was only the excessive air conditioning.

I head to the decontamination room and strip off the brightly colored baju kurung my grandmother laid out for me today. I've never had the heart to tell her none of my traditional clothes have ever made it past decontamination. I stand in the middle of the room, nude and shivering, as nozzles spray puffs of gaseous chemicals over my bare skin. A green light flashes and I hurry into sterilized lab garments before someone else barges in the room. Even after the past

67

few years, I still shudder at the lack of respect for privacy and modesty many of the foreigners show. I've never found out if this is just their way, or if they do not think women like me deserve the same treatment they give their own females.

But I escape the sting of humiliation today, if only by a few seconds—my sterile whites are completely in place by the time Dr. Whitlock shoves open the door. His mouth is pinched in a thin line.

"I need a protein analysis of test subject 642's sweat glands and hair follicles," he barks.

"I performed one yesterday. The results are listed in the…"

"Do it again." He turns and leaves, no explanation.

I sigh and make my way to the containment area where the test subjects are held. 642 is a female of mostly P. pygmaeus, common orangutan genotype, though like all the subjects here her genes have undergone extensive modifications. She is nearly hairless, and an albino, genetic modifications that make studying and caring for her easier. Her hairlessness makes her face look ancient and uncomfortably human. I try not to notice how she shivers in her cage. Her eyes leak constant tears, which I'm told is a genetic malfunction too minor to be of concern. I remind myself, again, that she's just an animal.

I signal her with the clicker, and 642 extends her arm. I scrape a few of her skin cells into a device Dr. Whitlock developed. Her skin is warm and crinkly, like my grandmother's. I give her another signal, and 642 allows me to pluck a few stringy hairs from her head, the only place on her body they still grow. I'm about to leave when she pats my arm and makes a soft hooting noise.

Startled, I ask her, "What is it?"

She hoots again and waves her hand in front of her face. Something is different about her. I hear the door open behind me. It's the head trainer, and he's carrying an electric prod.

"Step back," he says. He jams the prod into the cage. 642 screams once, then collapses, her limbs jerking. When he pulls the prod away, she lies still, helpless, covered in her own urine. I think for a moment he's killed her, but the monitors show a weak heartbeat.

The trainer smiles at me as though we've just shared a joke. "They've been getting restless lately. These mods-- well, the whole thing's a bad idea, if you ask me." He leers unpleasantly. I try not to cringe.

"I should finish with the samples," I say. The trainer nods and waves at me to go.

As I'm walking away, I think, her eyes. 642 was waving at her eyes. What did she mean? I shake my head. An animal, I think. Just an animal. Like me.

The foreigners said they would bring education to the villages. Knowledge, we had heard, would bring our people into the modern world. Our elders traded them land. Our men and women built the university and the labs.

But the foreigners charged a high price for their education, and no one in the village could afford to pay it. That's when the foreigners offered us a bargain. Knowledge and training, they said, in exchange for service. They would fund our schools and in exchange we would work in their companies and their labs. It's not the same as the debt slavery you had under the sultans, they said. Just sign the contract.

The contract no one could properly read or understand.

I had done well in school and came to their attention early. Scientific ability, they said. Very valuable. They gave me a pat on the head and sent me to work in the labs.

642, on the other hand, was one of the last of her kind. The others perished when the forest was razed before I was even born. My people had called her kind the "people of the forest," and had thought of them as near-human, like cousins. The foreigners agreed--the forest people were such close cousins they would make good test subjects, once they were modified, of course.

I analyze 642's skin and hair samples. The research Dr. Whitlock is conducting is top secret. A debt-bonded assistant like me is not supposed to know about it, much less understand it. But the genomic patterns fit together in my head like the intricate lines of embroidery my grandmother works into the clothes I'm never allowed to wear. I have not seen genetic material like this before, not human or P. pygmaeus.

I'm supposed to report anomalies. This time I don't.

Instead, I run a search of various DNA databases, trying to match the patterns. It won't be the first time Dr. Whitlock and his colleagues have experimented with genetic manipulation, adding non-primate genes to subjects' DNA and studying the results. But these genes don't match any in the database. Instead, they hardly seem like viable strands at all, more like floating disjunct fragments. Where did they come from? How are they holding together enough to even function?

I close my eyes, thinking. 642 swims in my mind's eye. Pasty white skin wrinkled with age and dimpled with cold. Albino. But not completely. Startled, I remember her strange gesture. Her eyes. Not pinkish albino red anymore, but a deep purple.

There were rumors about the foreigner's colony on a faraway moon. Rumors about alien DNA, an encounter (or encounters) with a mysterious creature from that strange place, or else visiting there from outside the solar system.

Stories about eyes and skin and hair that turned dark purple or blue.

I hear a loud clatter, and I jerk my eyes open. It's Haziq bin Rahman, a fellow tech. This week, he's been ordered to perform cleaning and sterilization duties as a punishment for insubordination.

Haziq bows in apology. "I am sorry to disturb you, Zulaikha Khan. I accidentally dropped the sample canisters."

I incline my head in courtesy. "Not at all, Doctor Rahman." He flushes at the sound of his title, which he has not been allowed to use yet. He bends over to pick up his canisters, glancing at the genetic sequences on the screen.

As he leaves, I hear him whisper, "Be careful, little sister." The warm sound of his voice passes over my skin like an electric current, but his warning sinks into my mind.

I email my analysis of subject 642's hair and skin samples to Dr. Whitlock, careful not to include any information or conjecture "off limits" to bonded techs. Before I receive his reply, my console goes blank, then blinks at me. Bright red letters run across the screen, summoning all lab techs to the theater.

I dispose of my samples and sterilize my equipment, then head to the theater. Dr. Whitlock is waiting outside the doors, his hair and coat in disarray for the first time I can remember. The bonded techs line up before him, and as we enter, he gives each of us an injection from a steri-gun. The cold touch of the gun makes me shiver at first, then I feel a stinging burn around the injection site. What are they giving us this time?

I file through with everyone else. The doors close behind us, and Dr. Whitlock hurries on stage to sit with several other high-ranking foreigners.

71

Dr. Ivanov rises to speak. "Contamination," he begins. Mutated virus. Possible security breaches. He speaks through gritted teeth, as though he'd like to bite us. My shoulder blades itch, like insects are crawling on the underside of my skin. There are murmurs around me. Are we going to be fired? they wonder. Or something worse?

"We've given you an immune booster and an experimental anti-viral," Ivanov continues. "We don't know if that will be enough to protect you."

He lays out the new order. No going home or leaving the lab until we've developed a vaccine or an effective treatment regimen. No messaging, phone calls, or communication with the outside world. Your families will be notified.

A hand in the air. Ivanov stops, staring. I turn to see who it is. Bonded techs follow orders, and asking questions is dangerous. My heart beats--it's Haziq, looking dignified despite the janitor's uniform they made him wear.

"What are the symptoms of this escaped virus? How can we know if one of us has it?" he asks.

Ivanov gives him a cold glare, then waves his hand in dismissal. But one of the other foreigners, a female, stands up.

"The virus was a vector," she says. "It delivered genetic modifications. Without the specific genes we used for therapeutic purposes, it could deliver any DNA strands of the correct size. It could cause cancers, genetic changes, any number of symptoms. It's impossible to predict its effects."

That is not true, I think. The vector viruses are highly specific, and the changes they make very predictable. I remember my parents, and the virus that killed them. I wonder what the foreigners have tampered with.

The unending shifts are dreary. Analyzing samples from a dozen different sources. Hours staring into an electron microscope, Dr. Whitlock barking orders. At night I collapse into a makeshift cot, warming my stiff fingers under my breath. I miss my grandmother, her fragrant yellow curries and cheerful prattle. She talked endlessly of matchmaking, and I listened, dreaming. We are not allowed to marry until the contract is fulfilled, and my contract stretched before me, eating up my marriageable years. I was as cold and sterile as the lab equipment.

The first person to die is a female foreigner. Blue and white streaks crisscross her skin and she screams about monsters inside her head. They take her to an isolation ward in the University hospital, but it's too late. Dr. Whitlock orders me to collect skin and hair samples from her corpse before her body is incinerated. I put on a gas-tight hazmat suit and go to look for her.

I find the foreign girl on an exam table in an empty ward. Though she had been a young woman, not much older than me, her skin is thin and wrinkled, sagging off her bones as though she'd wasted away for months or years, not days. There's an intubator still stuck in her throat.

In our village, the women of the family take care of the dead. My grandmother prepared my mother's corpse with tender care. She'd washed dried sweat from her own daughter's body, then carefully rinsed the last traces of vomit from my mother's mouth. At thirteen years old, I'd brushed out my mother's long black hair for the last time. I remember its softness and weight in my hands, and how I arranged it to hide the spots where some had fallen out from the sickness. We wrapped her in a crisp white sheet my grandmother had sewn with shimmering seed pearls. The whole village walked in the mourning procession for her and my father, singing prayers and songs. Even as grief stung my heart like the tentacles of a red jellyfish, I'd thought about how loved and honored my mother was. I hoped her spirit knew how deeply we missed her.

No one has performed any funeral rites for the dead foreigner. Her body is splayed out on the exam table, unwashed and undignified. I feel sorry for her, alone and abandoned in death. I pull out the intubator and do my best to wipe the blood off her face with my thickly gloved hand. It's foolish, I know. Is this any different than collecting samples from a lab animal? I think of 642, and my stomach lurches. Had the modded P. pygmaeus survived the recent rounds of tests, or was another lab assistant collecting samples from her limp form before dumping her in the incinerator?

I collect my samples. Skin, hair, blood. Spinal fluid. Selected organ tissues. Worst, the retinas from her eyes. The easiest way to collect these is to shear away the eyelid first. I've done it before, to animals. No one would complain or even notice if I did. She won't have a funeral.

I pinch her eyelashes between my fingers and lift the scalpel. But the slim knife feels heavy in my hands, and I put it down again. I cannot bear to degrade her body any more than it has been. I let go of her eyelid, but to my surprise her eye doesn't snap shut from rigor mortis. Instead, it stares at me, blood-red, unseeing. I frown and check her description. Eye color doesn't change after death, and no one reported her eyes had turned red. I open her other eye with my fingers. It's a violent blue, twice as vivid as the foreigners usually had. I scrape a few cells off each of her retinas, then close her eyes again. My samples collected, I head back to the lab for an analysis.

Under my breath, soft enough that the radio in my suit can't pick it up, I hum a mourning song for the strange girl who died far from her home.

The virus spreads. Foreigners and bonded techs alike fall ill and die within hours. Some of the high-level foreign scientists, including Dr. Ivanov and Dr. Whitlock, flee the lab. One or more of them carries the virus to the outside world, and the news reports roll in. The gen-plague, they call it, because those who survive often have permanent genetic mutations--albinism, strangely colored patches of skin or hair, malfunctioning organs.

There are protesters outside the lab, angry foreigners waving signs with gruesome pictures. I'm afraid to see my grandmother for fear of spreading the virus, but I have caught glimpses of her on news footage of the protests. She sits quietly on the ground, legs crossed, waiting. She looks at the cameras with a quizzical eye and ignores the foreigners' attempts to speak to her.

I miss her terribly, but there is so much to do, I can't think of her often. I help Haziq organize the lab into a makeshift hospital. Together, we care for sick techs as well as the few foreigners who'd stayed. Working by his side to help the sick, I feel more alive than I had since before my parents died. For the first time, I use my skills to help my own people, instead of doing nothing but blindly following the foreigners' orders like a rat in a maze. I study the chemical composition of the strange virus day after day, picking apart its genetics, looking for weaknesses, possible treatments, anything. Haziq tends the sick with warmth and compassion, trying drug after drug, all the regimens we could find in the foreigners' books and medicines.

Nothing works. The patients scream. Blotchy streaks of blue or purple or other wild colors spread across their skin, and their organs fail, one after another, in a hundred different patterns with the same result.

All my education, I think. For nothing.

"You mustn't blame yourself," Haziq tells me one day. I sit hunched over a microscanner, examining a model of the virus' RNA, turning it over in my mind like a mahjong piece, wondering how it fit.

I reach up to wipe a tear from my eye--a foolish, wasted gesture, as my gloved hand couldn't reach beneath the protective gear. Haziq catches my hand and holds it. I feel as though an electric current passed between us. Warmth spreads through my fingers.

"Zulaikha," Haziq whispers, and my heart opens like the bloom of a banyan tree.

"Yes," I say. He presses my hand to his chest and gives an awkward bow. "Yes, Haziq, my--"

Words die in my throat. "No," I say, "No, oh no..." It is on him. Bluish purple, like the dark waters of the sea in storm, spreading across the back of his neck.

His eyes widen, and his hand clutches at his chest. Already a thin line of blood trickles down his cheek, a blood tear, characteristic of the virus' late stages. He topples forward, and it is all I can do to keep him from falling.

I find a makeshift cot and some clean blankets for Haziq. He shivers in the artificial cold, still set to the foreigner's liking. I pace beside him. The computers are useless. Sequences of the virus' RNA, detailed analysis of its outer proteins--all of it tells me nothing of its treatment. Everything about it is carefully modeled to be a smooth and efficient vector for gene therapy, and none of it should cause these symptoms. And the traces of DNA I've found are broken, floating strands that look like nothing at all.

Nothing I can *see*, anyhow.

I stop pacing, my heart thudding in my ears. What couldn't I see?

I visit the animals in the laboratory to search for answers. 642 is still there. The foreigners must have bred her before they fled, because she is heavily pregnant. I adjust the automatic feeding machines to account for her condition, and she gobbles down the nutrient-rich mush the machine spits out.

How did you survive? I want to ask her. She blinks at me with her sad eyes, which are still a deep purple. She holds out her arm, as she used to when I came to her to take blood samples.

I shake my head, thinking. The anomalies in her blood had been like the ones in the virus. I'd never seen anything like them before. But what seemed like pieces had fit together in my mind, like a tapestry woven with a handful of invisible threads. What if the pieces were there, but I couldn't see them?

642 makes a gentle hooting sound. She pulls her arm back in the cage and finishes her mash. One arm curls protectively over her swollen belly.

There are nature reserves. Islands of trees in a concrete blight. They don't usually take lab animals, but I might find a way. There is no one left to stop me from trying.

I tap the cage. 642 offers her arm, and I take a vial of her blood, one last sample. I pat her arm when I'm done. It might be foolish to talk to a non-human animal. Dr. Whitlock would think so. But I don't care.

"When I have finished my other work," I tell her. "I'll try...I'll find a way to take you away from here. Someplace warmer. Kinder."

642 huffs. I don't know if she can understand me. I'm not sure it matters.

Back in the lab I compare the anomaly in 642's genetic material with the DNA from the virus. If 642's genome fits together like an intricate tapestry, the virus' look broken and torn, like someone has slashed it apart then hastily glued it back together.

The invisible threads are missing, I think. They tried to rip out what they didn't understand.

I close my eyes and try to repair it in my mind, to knit up ragged edges and bind the pieces of DNA back together. It's like trying to write on the sand as the tide is coming in.

I check on Haziq. He's shivering, soaked in cold sweat, and one of his eyes is blood-red, and the other an unearthly lavender. I fill a sink with warm, soapy water, and clean him as best I can. His breathing slows, and I hope it is because he is calmer and more comfortable. I wrap him in the warmest blanket I can find, tucking it around him. His eyelids, flicker, then close. I hold his hand.

There are important things you cannot see. The ties that bind us together, one person to another. They are invisible, but you can feel them.

I go back to the microscanner. I do not try to force the amino acids together. I search for the gaps, the shredded ends, the hollows of the missing sections. And I try to find the shapes that could fill them the bizarre, seemingly empty spaces from 642's DNA. But the spaces aren't empty, I realize. They can't be. The molecular mass is too great. They are there, but invisible to the scanner, no matter what spectrum I use to take the readings. Repairing the virus DNA is like painting blindfolded, feeling the contours of colors and shapes with fingers, not eyes.

My head hurts. I blink at the computer, and I don't know what time it is, or how long I've been working. I struggle from my chair, bone-weary. I am not allowed to use the molecular nano-printer, but Dr. Whitlock's encryption is easy to break. I do not know if this will work, and there is no time to test it. It might be too late anyway, at least for Haziq. That thought makes my insides churn and my blood go cold as dark space. I force myself to move slowly, methodically. No room for mistakes.

The nano-printer spits out a vial of orange liquid. I load it into a steri-gun. I will not let my fingers tremble.

What if I'm wrong? He will die, and many more. If I've made it worse, they could all die, choking and screaming and burning, fever-mad.

I could search the labs for a leftover P. pygmaeus, or even use 642. No, I won't do that. Never again. I hold the gun to my arm. I could test it on myself, observe the results. But I don't have time.

I don't know how I know, but I do. I rush from the lab, find him, hold him. He weeps in my arms like a babe. I kiss him gently, reassuring. And I inject the orange vial into his neck.

The world slumbers. Stars shine. I had thought it would all end, that our fate would be written across the sky of a broken world, but that is not how it works. The cold expanse of the cosmos stretches out around me, as quiet as the last breath of the dying, and its beauty cracks against my ribs.

642 snores peacefully in the back of a stolen truck, her newborn infant cradled in her arms. No one would have let me take them only a few days ago, but hours ago a guard

kissed both my hands and pressed the keys into my limp fingers. Then he knelt begged for the honor of driving me. I nodded blankly. I have never driven a car.

The forest is an island, lush and loud and verdant in a desert of plantations that surround it like a hostile army. But it survives, and a raucous chorus greets the thing grey fingers of dawn.

I could notify the wardens about 642. There might even be a sanctuary specific to P. pgymaeus nearby. But I don't. Given her unique genetic signature, they'd never let her be. She'd be hunted, her babe trapped in a cage, as she had been. And unlike most lab animals, I have a sense that she will be capable of taking care of herself and her babe without human interference.

"It is time," I say, gently patting her shoulder. Her eyes blink open, a vivid electric blue, and I don't look at them to long or too closely, because I can't bear to look at eyes like those for very long. Haziq had the clarity of the dying. He forgave my failure.

"Shhh," he'd said. "Beloved...there are so many others, Zulaikha, and you will save them. I am just too far gone." When I close my eyes, I feel the clasp of his hand in mine. A swell of grief threatens to overtake me.

642 hoots softly. Her babe squirms against her chest. He is strong, and I can tell that his bright eyes are already scanning the forest, taking it in, relishing its wild glory. One day, he will be its fierce protector.

I watch as they disappear in the trees, then slump against the truck. My driver waits silently, and something about the way his hands curl against the steering wheel calls me back. His mother rose from her cot today after I gave her the treatment I'd made. She was weak and shivering, but her heartbeat was strong. So many people need me, and I cannot abandon them.

I climb into the backseat.

"Where should I take you now, Honored Sister?" he asks.

"The lab," I say. "There is much to do."

ALEXIS LANTGEN

EARTH IS FOR EARTHERS

I was born a year after the Europa colonies collapsed, so I don't remember how the tragedy tore apart the old U-Fed. I don't remember having the gen-plague either. I caught it at age three, supposedly from a GMO strawberry plant someone gave my mother as a gift. Rose-li, my older sister, told me that they gave me all the popsicles I could eat, until my mouth and chin turned a deep bluish purple from all the juice. Rose-li wasn't so lucky. The plague spores settled in her lungs, and she spent months in a hospital struggling to breathe. In my first memory of her, she's leaning against a bookshelf in the children's ward, an oxygen mask strapped across her face. She turned pages for me and pointed at pictures, unable to speak.

Mama had a miscarriage while Rose-li was still in the hospital, and my father blamed the plague. After that, he carried Mama's strawberry plant in the bright green pot to our backyard. He set it on an old fence post and stared at it. Then he smashed it to pieces with a tire iron. He hit it again and again, long after the pot was crushed into chalky powder. Strawberry pulp was splattered across the post, blood-red.

Mama watched him destroy her plant. She covered her face with her hands and peered out between her fingers, her mouth working. When he came inside, she brought him a drink and waited until he started sipping it before she spoke.

"W-w-why, Thomas? They didn't get sick from the berries, or you and me would've got it, too. I thought it was probably the milk or--"

"Shut your trap." He crushed the soda can she'd given him in his fist and hurled it in a corner. Mama jumped and clapped a hand over her mouth, careful to keep her words from escaping again.

He glared at her. "We're not going to have any of that unnatural crap in this house ever again. You buy pure food and real plants, not some fancy berry that don't need soil or pest spray. No modded shit." The veins in his neck bulged, and Mama nodded.

He wasn't alone in his thinking back then, of course. Gen-mods became a taboo after the plague. Then they found the survivors from Europa--twelve years after the life support systems had failed.

That I remember clear as sheet ice--they were all over the vids. At first, the Federation wouldn't say how they'd survived, just that a few people had withstood the cosmic radiation, shattering cold, and thin atmosphere long enough to return to Earth. But the truth leaked, and soon everyone knew that the Europans had modded themselves, altered their own DNA to survive.

I watched the first vids of the Europans' chosen representatives, my eyes glued to the screen. They had the shape of normal Earthers, but their skin was royal purple or midnight blue, and their hair grew in thick, flat strands of chitin. They had tremulous smiles and awkward hands, and they blinked under glaring light of a thousand video cameras. I wondered if they had any children who'd survived the mods and escaped the plague. I thought about what it would be like to meet a Europan girl my age.

At first it looked like I might have the chance to make a Europan friend--the Federation chose to resettle some of the rescued Europans in our district. But the day they arrived, my father dragged me out of bed early and made me put on a T-shirt he'd made with an ugly drawing of the Europans on it, one that made them look like aliens or monsters. He took me down to the hoverport where we stood with a crowd of angry men waving signs. One read, "Go Back To Wear You Came From, Freaks."

"Don't they come from Earth?" I asked. "They're survivors from an Earth colony."

"That's what the Feds want you to think," my father said as he handed me a sign. "I've heard they're really aliens that killed the original colonists and took their places. And even if they used to be humans, they're filthy, unnatural gen-mods now." He pressed his lips together in a frown I knew too well.

I shut my mouth and looked at the sign he'd given me. "People, Not Purps. Earth for Earthers." I held it out at arm's reach, as if I'd only happened to pick it up by accident. My father screamed slogans so loud that spit flew out of his mouth. Then I saw the Europans.

The first ones out of the hovercraft were two men and a woman. They held each other's hands and stared straight ahead, as though they couldn't see us--or wouldn't look at us. More and more of them came out of the craft, and they joined hands with the others, making a loose circle. My father and the rest of the angry crowd around us stopped screaming. They milled around, watching the Europans.

"What's all this bullshit?" my father muttered. He glared at one of the young Europan women until his eyes bulged. A tremor passed through her body, but she kept staring straight ahead.

There was a pause as though everyone held their breath, the Europans and the protesters. One of the Europans, a tall woman with skin like blue twilight, turned and nodded at the men closest to the hovercraft. One of the men gave a low whistle, and small purple heads peeked out of the hatch. There were children with them after all--gaggle of kids all ages lead by a skinny teenage boy.

When the children emerged from the hovercraft, the Europans drew closer together, surrounding them. The crowd worked themselves up again, hisses and jeers growing louder and louder. The blue Europan woman raised her hands, and I thought she intended to quell the crowd. Instead, all the Europans started to sing. It wasn't a tune I recognized--Rose-li told me later it was an anthem from the old U-Fed. But they sang it loudly enough to drown out the angry yells.

My father's lip curled into a sneer. He jerked my arm towards our rusted roadcar. I dragged my feet, eager to see more of the Europans. But when the veins in my father's neck bulged like that, I knew better than to protest.

When we got home, I waited until my father trudged into the house to make my escape. I bolted down the street so fast the wind whipped against my face, stinging my eyes. I didn't dare turn around until I felt the rough bark of my favorite tree beneath my hands. It stood next to an old abandoned house at the end of our street, an ancient hazel with a thick, gnarled trunk and spreading branches that hid me from the outside world.

I closed my eyes and breathed in its warm, nutty smell. A loud crack--like a door being slammed--made me jump. I pressed my face against the bark until my trembling stopped. When the green space around me grew still enough I could hear the soft hum of the synth-bees, I gripped the tree's lower limbs and hoisted myself into the canopy. One of the upper branches had a comfortable bend I'd rubbed smooth from years of climbing. I kept a sketchpad and a stash of books in a nearby hollow, safe in a water-tight lock-cloth.

I pulled out my sketchpad first--I wanted to draw a portrait of the Europan woman I saw earlier. The way her chin lifted when she sang captivated me. But then I remembered the ugly alien drawings from the signs, and I put my pencil down. I couldn't bear it if my drawing looked like that. I'd put away my drawing materials and pulled out my favorite book when I heard a rustling at the base of the tree. My throat closed up, and I went still. I heard a soft "ooph" and felt the leaves tremble. Someone else at the base of my tree, pulling themselves up the branches.

"Kendy? Are you there?" It was my sister, Rose-li. I let out my breath when I saw her white hair peeking through the leaves beneath me. I reached down to help her onto the upper branches. Rose-li may have been four years older than me, but the gen-plague slowed her growth. We were the same size, though I was wiry from running and climbing, and she was thin and frail. Our faces had the same shape though, so much that our neighbors might have thought we were identical twins if not for Rose-li's eyes and hair. The plague caused random gen-mods that stole the color from her hair and skin, so that she looked albino, except for her eyes. Those deepened into a midnight blue so dark it could have been black. She was strange and beautiful and unearthly, like an elf or a visitor from the stars.

"How bad was it?" I asked.

"He broke all those perfume bottles Aunt Margie sent you for Liberty Day. No one told him how much you hated them." She gave me a Cheshire Cat grin. "Did you meet any Europans?"

"You know I didn't," I said, flicking a lost pollinator drone off my leg.

"I did." She twirled a tendril of fine white hair around her fingers. "They got here after he went to work. Moved in next door."

"Mad mechanics, he'll fry his motherboard."

"I hope not," Rose-li said. A flush creeped up her cheeks. She leaned back on her favorite branch and stared up at the sky. We used to spend hours watching the clouds, fluffy and white as cotton balls. I miss them sometimes, even they aren't as spectacular as geomagnetic storms.

I should have asked Rose-li then what the blush was about. Maybe I could have stopped what happened if I'd known what she was thinking. Maybe I could have saved her.

But I didn't. I leaned back on my branch, and we talked about the things that seemed important to me then.

Over the next couple months, Rose-li avoided the house. That didn't surprise me though; my father was as vicious and jumpy as a wildcat on meth. Even today, I have scars that crisscross my back from the time he caught me reading a book by one of the Europans.

"You filthy little bitch," he said.

I huddled on the floor, my shirt in tatters around me. Burning welts studded their way across my flesh. I pressed my cheek to the floor, and sweaty hair fell like a curtain over my eyes. I never saw his face, only his sludgy work boots as they crossed the floor to where my book lay open. Its clean white pages fluttered like the wings of a bird. He ground his boot into it, crushing the binding beneath his heel. I heard the sound of a zipper. A stream of hot piss splattered over my book, leaving yellow streaks like a trail of acidic tears.

He left after that. The book was ruined. I picked it up from the least-nasty corner. I couldn't bear to just throw it away, as battered and foul-smelling as it was. That night, I buried it at the foot of my tree, as though it was a beloved pet.

My skin prickled in the chill air. I had a terrible sense of foreboding. Perhaps it was the red-tinged moon, like a bloody fist in the sky. A lunar eclipse, which the ancients considered a sign of doom.

An eerie feeling stole over me, like I was being watched. I heard a giggle from the branches overhead.

"Rose-li?" I called. So far as I knew, she was the only one who knew about my tree. On the other hand, I'd never heard my sister giggle like that.

Another giggle. "Come on up!" Rose-li called, her voice soft and sweet as the solar wind over the crystalline snows.

I climbed towards my accustomed branch, but before I got there, I felt dangling legs. Someone else was in my spot. Someone whose legs were thicker and heavier than Rose-li's by far.

"What?! Who are you?" I said. I could make out the stranger's outline, but his features were lost in the night, as though he was part of the sky. Rose-li, on the other hand, glowed in the moonlight.

"Over here," she said, and she pulled me onto a branch next to her. "This is Arion." The shadow nodded at me. His eyes shone in the dark like a cat's.

I gasped. "You're Europan!" His skin was the dark blue of deep water.

He laughed. "Please don't run screaming."

"I won't," I said, even though I knew he was joking. Pieces of a puzzle fell together, and I felt a sharp knife of fear in my chest. I looked at Rose-li's shining eyes. "This is where you've been sneaking off to."

"Yes," she said. "We met the day he moved in." Rose-li turned her face to the stars, and her black eyes seemed to glimmer in their light. Arion ran a hand over her wild tangle of milk white hair and brushed her lips with a gentle kiss.

"We're going to Europa," she told me. "Arion has the gen-mods so I can be like them. He wanted to see Earth, but now that he's here..."

"I get it," I said.

"There are fields of ice crystals like giant snowflakes, and Jupiter rises over the horizon like a red-gold sun, and Dad will never find us there, we'll be free and happy and ..." She looked at Arion as though he were the sun, and her lips had the sweet, peaceful smile of pure contentment. He touched her skin with wonder and reverence, a like a moon-struck prince from a fairytale.

"Everything's ready--transport, identicards. Can't bring many personals on the ships anyway, so we don't need to pack anything," Arion said. He had a platinum starbox that he wore around his neck. He opened it up to show me a long lock of moonlight hair. When he pressed a button, the box projected an image of Rose-Li, waving at him from our upstairs window.

"To remember how you looked the first time I saw you," he said to my sister.

"Will you still love me when I'm all purple?" she said, laughing.

"Forever," he said. He pressed another button on the starbox. Its sides folded down to reveal an iridescent crystal ring. He slipped it on her finger. It glowed softly against her skin.

Rose-li opened her mouth, then shut it again. Then she wrapped her arms around Arion's neck and kissed him.

I wanted to be happy for them, my sister the moon-maiden and her lover the star traveler. But I remembered my buried book and trembled.

"Let Mom and Dad know where I've gone," Rose-li told me. "I was going to leave a note, but maybe they'll feel better hearing it from you. But not until the cruiser leaves, a few days from now. I'm going to take the gen-mods tomorrow night, so I'll be ready. Can you cover for me for a while?"

"I'll try," I told her. I wanted to warn her about father, but she knew his rage as well as me. If she was willing to take this kind of risk, their love had to be as deep and mad as galactic space.

I knew something was up with *him* when I woke up the next day to a silent house. I'd expected Rose-li to be gone, but it was his day off, which he normally spent muttering in front of the vids drinking beer. My mother had left a note that she was going to visit my aunt.

I usually loved silence. It meant I could read or run free without looking over my shoulder. But this silence felt heavy, as though even the drones held their breath. I tried to read but found myself staring at the pages in frozen stillness, like a rabbit waiting in the crushing iron jaws of a trap. I was almost relieved to hear distant hollers as evening fell.

I didn't want to go, but my feet drew me near the ruckus. It came from the greenspace past the end of our street. It looked like another anti-Europan rally like the one my father made me go to. Men slurped cans of beer and stood around a bonfire. A few of them wore masks, but most had brazened grins on bare faces. The fire cast lurid shadows over them all, until their features seemed twisted and grotesque. Young boys threw sticks in the fire or ran around the trees playing aliens and spacemen. They cornered a stray dog and took turns hitting it.

"Die, gene-freak, die!" one boy screamed, spit flying from his mouth. He whipped the dog until it howled and its flanks ran with blood. One of the older men laughed.

I saw a few women there--middle-aged friends of my mother's and an elderly neighbor who once dragged me to my father for punishment after I broke her flowerpot. They'd set up a potluck on a nearby picnic table and sat around like they were about to watch an Astro Show.

Everything looked so ordinary; the familiar faces, the potluck, the bonfire. I wanted to believe in it. It was a warm night, but I shuddered as though someone had dropped a snowball down the back of my shirt. Everyone around me looked full of anticipation and excitement, eager for...what? My throat closed--I didn't want to know--I needed to leave...

Too late. My father's voice rooted me to the ground. I trembled. He had that tone, the one that promised violence, controlled rage. But it wasn't my name he was calling.

When I brought myself to look at him, I saw he stood on two picnic tables jammed together into a makeshift platform. The crowd rallied around him, shaking their fists in the air. I was wrong about controlled rage. He howled like a wild beast, spittle flying from his mouth, his words lost in fury. As he waved his arms like a madman, I saw it failing around on its chain, dangling from his fist.

Arion's starbox.

"Filth!" my father screamed. "Lecher! Rapist! Animal!"

How could he have gotten it? Arion would never have given it to him. Could they have accidentally left it behind? No, they weren't supposed to leave yet, Rose-li wouldn't take the gen-mods until tonight.

I stood on my toes, craning to look over the crowd. A hand clamped around my wrist like a vice.

"You're his daughter," a man said. He wore lurid red mask, but I recognized his voice. He lived in the neighborhood--I'd played starcruiser with his children. Now he loomed over me, his breath stinking of alcohol. He squeezed my wrist until my bones were grinding together. "You Rose-li?"

"No, Kendy," I said.

"Come with me," he said, relaxing his grip on my wrist. I didn't dare disobey or fight back. He took me to the platform where my father stood. There was a large dog kennel covered in a heavy tarp near the platform. I didn't see Rose-li or Arion.

"It's time!" my father shrieked. "We need to show those freaks that this is our planet! Earth for Earthers!" The crowd cheered. Some of the men got hold of the kennel and lifted it on to the platform by my father.

"It's time they learn that there's a difference between humans and gen-modded alien freaks!" my father yelled. He pulled the tarp off the kennel like a magician performing a trick.

A man lay huddled in the kennel. A Europan. Blood crusted the strips of chitin on his head, red and black against deep blue skin. Arion.

He lifted his head. One of his eyes had swollen shut, and the other shone in the dark like a tiny moon. When he saw me, he gave me a slight smile, as if to reassure me it would be alright. Then his eye blinked closed. Could he be winking at me? Why?

Father loomed over the kennel. "This beast," he said in a hushed voice that frightened me more than all his screaming. "This beast was *watching* my daughter. Perhaps he thought she would succumb to his animal desires since she was damaged by that foul plague."

He pressed the halo button on Arion's starbox. Rose-li's image appeared. The crowd gasped. My father pressed the button again and pulled out the lock of Rose-li's hair.

"When did you take this, beast?" he asked Arion, rattling the kennel bars. "How did you get it? Did you rape my baby? Did you foul her with your sick lusts?"

Arion opened his mouth to speak, but his words were lost in the howl of the crowd.

"Kill It! Kill It!" they screamed.

How many of them, I wondered, had turned their backs when Rose-li walked by, afraid of the mutations the genplague left on her? How many looked the other way when I had another black eye, or wore long sleeves all summer to cover my bruises?

"He didn't do anything!" I yelled. "It's not like that! She loves him!" No one heard me over the roar of the crowd, or if they did, they didn't listen. The man in the red mask tightened his grip and twisted my arm behind my back until I bent over in pain.

Things moved fast, too fast. My father had a length of metallic grey wire coiled like a snake. He looped one end, twisting it into a noose. He tossed the other end over a gnarled tree branch. Other men caught it and pulled it taunt. I screamed and struggled. Arion lay there, his eyes closed. Did he pass out? No more pain, I hoped. No more pain.

My father smashed his foot through the kennel door, nearly knocking it off the table. "Are you a coward too, filth? Did you faint like a fucking chicken when you saw your death?" He ground his heel into Arion's face, just as he'd done with my book. Then he looped the wire over Arion's neck and lifted his limp body into a standing position. In a bizarre way, my father looked almost tender, holding the Europan boy up and lifting his head.

"Did you think I'd allow you to touch my baby girl?" My father asked, looking straight into Arion's beaten face. Arion's head fell sideways, and his arms splayed out. My father spat on him, then hurled his body off the platform.

If my father intended to snap Arion's neck, he failed. The men holding the rope were surprised by his throw. The wire slipped through their fingers, and Arion's body hit the ground with a hollow thunk. His eyelids fluttered, and blood trickled out of his mouth. A hush fell over the crowd.

"What are you waiting for? Haul him up!" my father said. The men gripped the wire again and pulled. They heaved him up until Arion's body dangled from the branch. The wire cut into the skin of his neck and his eyes bulged. His fingers twitched, then went still.

I writhed against my captor, then slumped forward, too sick to fight anymore. My tears crusted into streaks of burning salt. *Rose-li*, I thought, and my head hung forward. How could I tell her?

A murmur swept through the crowd, and they parted in front of me. My sister came through, brittle and fragile as a crystal of ice. When they saw her, the men holding Arion dropped their wire, and his body tumbled forward like a broken doll. She knelt beside him and cradled his head in her hands. No one moved. It was as if the crowd held their breath.

Rose-li slipped her fingers beneath the wire embedded in Arion's throat. It was embedded in his neck, and she eased it off him. Bits of flesh clung to the wire, but only a small amount of blood. She pressed her fingers against his neck, as though searching for a pulse. She put her ear to his chest, listening. Her face crumpled. She made a sound like the moan of sea ice before it cracks and splits. She covered his mouth with hers, driving her breath into his body, pushing on his chest and lifting his eyelids. But his chest never rose. His body stayed still and silent, and when his eyelids opened, he had the empty stare of death. Rose-li stopped her frantic movements. She closed his eyes and kissed each of his lids.

She smoothed Arion's chitin hair out of his face and brushed his forehead and lips with another kiss. She didn't look once at my father or at the crowd that silently watched her. She looked up once at the sky. The moon, cold and white as bone. The stars that would have been her home.

She looked at me, too, her eyes like the deep night sky. If I could have stopped her... But I didn't. She was fast. A sharp knife from our own kitchen. She probably brought it in case she needed to free him or fight her way over to him. Or maybe she knew before she got here--they wouldn't escape together. Not alive.

Sharp and fast. It slid into her body as though her skin parted for it in welcome. She drove it into her chest to its hilt.

96

Then she fell over her beloved, and her hair scattered over his body like a fall of snow.

It wasn't until then that the man in the red mask released me. I fell on my knees. I didn't scream or cry. My throat closed up. My hands gripped the grass, and I felt like the world was spinning so fast it was going to hurl me into space.

I saw my father step off his platform. He seemed unsteady on his feet, but that might have been because I couldn't focus my eyes. He knelt by Rose-li's body and touched her face with a tenderness I'd never seen from him before. He dropped Arion's starbox in the ground beside her then stumbled away.

After that, people faded into the darkness. Their feet scraped and skittered like frightened mice as they went home to pretend they hadn't seen anything. Then there was no sound but rustling leaves and the cries of a lonely bird.

I crawled over to my sister. Blood spread in a sticky pool beneath her, and her skin was cool. I thought about lying down beside her and Arion, staying there with them forever. I'd never go home again, and I had no other place. No other friends.

But something strange was happening. Arion's chest started to rise and fall. He coughed. I jerked back, shaking. He hadn't been breathing or had a pulse a moment ago. What was happening? I was going mad.

He shivered and his eyes fluttered open. "Rose-li?" he said, and he ran a hand over her white silk hair.

"Arion?" I gasped. "You're alive? What's going on?"

He furrowed his brow and blinked, still petting my sister's hair. "Moonflower, why are you so cold?" He wrapped his arms around Rose-li's corpse. "You must have been so worried..." He stopped and stared down at my sister, pressing

97

her limp body to his chest. Her head fell back. He pulled one of his hands away. In the moonlight, her blood glistened.

"Please, come with me, Arion. We'll go to Europa. They won't hurt you there. She wouldn't want you to stay here!" I said. I didn't know how he was alive, but I had to get him away from here before anyone came back.

"Rose-li, my Rosie...what happened?" Blood everywhere. Arion pressed his hands against the wound in her chest, but her life blood already soaked the ground.

"She thought you were dead," I said. "How did you survive?"

"The mutations . . . we torpor when we can't get air . . ." He rocked back and forth, clutching her to him, his whole body quivering. "She didn't know. It's my fault." He howled as though something inside him had cracked and splintered into a thousand lacerating shards.

I stopped pleading and let go of his arm. I couldn't save him.

I stared at the night sky. It was still early enough that I could find the planet Jupiter, brighter than any star. I wished I could go there, to Europa. What did Earth have for me anymore?

Arion's keening grew hoarse, then died away into a sob. He lay back down, cradling Rose-li's body to his. I heard his breath slow. He'd go back to sleep and stay that way forever.

"It's not your fault," I said. "I'm so sorry, I tried to..."

"I know." He sounded quiet and ragged, as though each word tore small pieces of his voice away. "Kendy?"

"Yes?"

"Rose-li's identicard and her boarding pass for the Europan shuttle--she'd want you to have them." He dug into his pocket and handed them to me.

"I don't look enough like her--"

"The mutation pod. It's in my basement. No one else is there--they fled when they heard...I'm the only one who stayed. You just have to get in it. The mods take three days."

"I'll be a Europan," I whispered.

"You'll be free," he said. "If that's what you want. You don't have to go back. She'd want..." His voice trailed away, but his mouth kept working, contorting in silent grief. He lifted one hand. The star box rested in his palm. "Take it," he breathed.

The star box gleamed in the moonlight, as beautiful and delicate as a platinum flower. I took it and slipped the chain around my neck.

"Thank you."

"Don't forget her," he said. "She deserves to be remembered." He stroked Rose-li's hair and kissed her. His eyes drifted shut. His breath slowed, then stopped. A sleep like death. I left them there, sleeping forever, Endymion and Selene. I hope they dream of each other.

I made my way down empty streets to Arion's house. It was near enough to my old house that I could see the lights through the windows. I didn't go any closer, though, or look long enough to see if my mother was home. I went into Arion's basement. The pod was there, pulsing and humming, its soft fronds undulating like ocean grasses. I stripped off my filthy clothes. I held out my hands, looking for the last time at my skin in its original color, rosy and freckled, too much like my father's.

When I emerged three days later, I'd turned a rich royal purple. I felt as beautiful as an evening star and as strong and agile as a wild cat. My hair was not like Arion's though, or like any other Europan's I'd seen. It fell in long strips, soft as fresh grass, white as bone. Pale as the moon. Like my sister.

YOU'LL BE SO MUCH CALMER

Jaylon jerked awake, panting. His sheets were tangled around him, soaked in sweat. He could not remember his dreams--never could, really--but this one must've been bad. He blinked at the soft green numbers at the top of his wallscreen. It was hours before he'd have to rise for work in the morning. He considered lying back down and trying to still the frantic rhythm of his pulse, but the sight of his twisted bed sheets made him shudder. Sleep wouldn't come again.

He dragged himself out of bed and shut off all the floor-to-ceiling screens that inhabited every room in his apartment. The house AI monitored him through the screens, and if it noticed him out of bed so early, it would ask him questions in a tone of computerized concern. He couldn't bear the thought of its chirpy electronic voice disrupting his quiet this morning, of all mornings. He pushed those thoughts away and focused on making himself a cup of coffee. It wasn't easy without the automation--he barely remembered the steps his father had shown him so long ago. But he persevered. He spilled ground coffee across the counter-tops and into his mug, but the resulting cup was dark and rich. He sipped it and leaned against the window, his forehead pressed against the glass.

Jaylon paid handsomely for the view from his apartment, but he seldom looked at it. Now he watched dawn's pink and orange fingers push away the blue-black night. The sun peaked above the trees at the far end of the park. They looked cool and inviting. He wished he'd taken the time to walk there, to enjoy the morning air under real trees before . . .

He shook his head. He could still go, he told himself. Nothing would stop him. But the tightness in his chest told him it was not to be. That part of his life--the adventurous part, the natural part--was over, or would be over, by five o'clock today. He tried to swallow, but his throat closed, and he spit his coffee back in the cup.

I could do it one last time, he thought. He considered going back to bed, finding old pictures of Lossanah and... And what? he wondered bitterly. It's an overcooked noodle, limp and pasty from the required treatments, small and scared and... impotent. Useless, the council AIs called it. An unnecessary appendage. It's so much better to be free of it, the screen had told him, its voice a low, soothing hum. It causes unnecessary irritation, hormone fluctuations. Males are much calmer and happier when it's gone. Jaylon wondered how much a machine understood happiness.

His shoulders sagged and the cup in his hand slipped out of his fingers and clattered against the floor. He didn't pick it up. Instead his hands clawed at the window pane, the cold, smooth unbreakable glass. He sank to his knees and howled like an animal.

"Master Jaylon! Your distress has awakened us. Perhaps you would like a tall glass of Hedron's SSRI elixir, which is filled with all the nutrients your brain needs to fight depression, and has a more satisfying taste than other SSRI elixirs?" A drone the size and shape of a frisbee hovered near Jaylon's head, its voice modulated to express sympathy. He remembered when the company AIs gave those out--*fun, new toys! Like personal robot butlers!* They didn't mention the ads. Or the surveillance.

Jaylon curled into a ball on the floor, tears running down his face. "I won't do it," he said. "Tell them I won't. It's hideous, I'm a man, fuck them all."

The drone came closer, and Jaylon noticed its edges were surprisingly sharp. It whirred. "You have already discussed this with the Prime Axon. Why have you changed your mind?" It clicked, and Jaylon knew it was videotaping him, broadcasting his words and image to...someone. Or something. He wondered what really happened to all the information it collected.

"I won't do it," he said again. This time he whispered. "It's not right..."

"But it is right for you," the drone replied. Its sympathetic tone transformed into a dark, low sound that somehow bore into his skull. "Humans decided that reproduction must be vigorously controlled to prevent genetic diseases, unpleasant color variations, and weaknesses. We have already purified over a billion undesirables from the population."

"Purified?"

"Removed their reproductive capability, among other measures. In some cases, the Axon uses their gametes for research as well. Your genome has many unusual genetic markers, so it's possible your testes will be used for this purpose. It would be a great honor for you."

Jaylon wiped his face with a clenched fist. "But w-w-why take the...the other..."

"Ahhh, I see. You are concerned about losing a source of pleasure. Remember that you are required to make sacrifices for the corporation, Master. In fact, when you signed your employment documents--"

"I just signed what they told me! Those documents were seven thousand pages long! They can't...I'm a man!" Jaylon slammed his fists against the smooth window, but it didn't break. He stared down at his knuckles, which were swollen and bloody.

"You are right, of course, Master. You may refuse the procedure. But your employment would be terminated, and your company housing, transportation and benefits canceled. And of course, you would greatly displease the Prime Axon." A dull metallic gleam reflected off the drone's razor-edge, like a mechanical smile. Jaylon pulled himself to his feet, unsteady and awkward, defiance drained away.

"A wise choice, Master. Your display of emotion indicates the necessity of the procedure. Even with high doses of mood-stabilizing enhancements, you still suffer from irritations, irrationality, and unsatisfied desire common to males of your status." The drone must have calibrated its voice to the exact pitch and inflection of the human emotion "unbearably smug." It focused its camera eyes on him, no doubt recording his reaction.

Jaylon held his breath and let his face go blank. After a moment, the drone whirred over to the broken coffee cup and suctioned up the pieces. Then it flew to its docking bay where it would upload its data to the Prime Axon. Along the way, it turned on all the wallscreens. Perhaps intending to calm him, the drone had set the screens to images of kittens playing in sunlit fields.

Jaylon leaned against the window and stared at his knuckles. He'd bandaged her hand that night. Lossanah. She'd shown up at his place, blood trickling down her lip, her wild black hair floating around her like a storm cloud.

"One of them grabbed me," she said when he saw the deep tears in the flesh of her wrist. "I jerked away from it and ran. By then they were firing rubber bullets and tear gas into the crowd, and the drones--"

"Why the fuck would you do something that stupid!" he'd yelled at her, his voice cracking. His hands shook as he dabbed her wounds with Hedron's Anti-Bacterial, Anti-Viral Healing Ointment. She winced.

"You know why, Jay." She sounded so quizzical, puzzled by his reactions. "They're going to start the operations next month if we don't stop them. It's sick!"

"You don't even want kids!" he hissed at her. He kept a towel pressed on her largest cut, the one that wouldn't stop bleeding.

"That's not the point! I should be able to choose for myself if I want them or not. Those fucking machines shouldn't get to--"

"Are you kidding me? You're the one who's always going on about all the assholes who abuse their kids or have ones they can't afford, or--"

"The answer isn't forcibly sterilizing people! It's like Nazi Germany or Communist China or--"

"Spare me. Nazis! Good god, it's about having a decent fucking society. It's about civilization. It's about only breeding the strongest and the best."

"Yeah, because that doesn't sound at all like what the Nazis were trying to do." She pulled her hands away from him, staring him down with the one eye she had that wasn't swollen shut. "I'm going to crash at Halima's tonight."

He shrugged his shoulders and kicked at the carpet. When she left, he threw her things into a box to give to her the next time he saw her. But he didn't see her. Not for months. Not at the university, not at her favorite bookstore, not at the coffee shop where she sometimes played for open mic nights. He tried not to think about her, but he couldn't shake the cold emptiness he felt in the pit of his stomach.

He'd nearly convinced himself he was over her, when a control drone called him out of one of his classes. It loomed over him like a fat mechanical spider the size of a car. It focused its sonic beams on him, and he felt its deep voice resonate through his body.

"Take us to her things," it said. It hadn't needed to say her name. Jaylon had swallowed. When he didn't answer immediately, the drone caught his waist in a vicious metal pincher. He'd felt his feet leave the ground. When they arrived at his apartment, he took the hulking drone straight to the box, *her* box. It dumped the contents into its gunmetal maw. When it finished, it turned its glowing red eyes on him.

"Report to wallscreen for interrogation," it said. It hovered over him, and he spilled his guts. Everything he knew about her, her family, their relationship, her friends--it bled out of him. Their intimate moments, his deepest feelings. When he was done, he threw up.

"Interrogation complete. Answers accepted. Citizen Jaylon will report for assignment at..." He barely heard the rest. When he managed to pull himself out of bed the next day, he discovered he'd been awarded a prestigious position at a top company in his field. He never saw Lossanah again.

He'd tried, over the years, to convince himself that everything was fine. The drones grew smaller, their voices became perky and unassuming. The companies assured everyone there were adequate protections in place to protect humans from machine overreach. Some days he'd even imagined that Lossanah was just fine somewhere--maybe the machines were looking for her because they were concerned. But when the Prime Axon, a control AI, told him to report for purification surgery, he felt the same terrible sickness he'd felt the day the drone came for her things.

Now there was no escape. If he ran, they'd catch him. If he refused, they'd punish him and likely force him to undergo the surgery anyway. He shuddered.

He forced himself to take a shower, but he couldn't bring himself to eat. Despite his early morning, he arrived to work late. He couldn't concentrate on anything and gave up trying after an hour. Instead he sat in his work cell and stared at the blinking wallscreens, his eyes wide and unseeing.

When the work surveillance drone tapped his shoulder, he jerked. It flashed pale blue lights at him, which he guessed were intended to be soothing.

"We are ready for you now, Citizen Jaylon," it said, in a voice pitched to sound soothing and kind. Jaylon nodded, his face empty.

When he tried to stand, he found his legs didn't work. The drone extended its robotic arm to steady him. It led him down a crooked hall to a room he'd never seen before. A tall medidrone stood in the corner, by a flat surgical table. His eyes slid away from the table and he focused on the medidrone instead. It reminded him of a refrigerator, until its compartments slid open to reveal an array of mechanical arms. He noticed it was the same gunmetal grey as the drone that had consumed Lossanah's things.

"Walk forward and lay back on the table, Citizen Jaylon," the work drone chirped.

His knees shook. It prodded him, and he started forward, then stopped again. He noticed restraints, chrome and leather, and bile rose in his throat. He turned to run, but the medidrone shot out its arms, clamping one around each of his limbs. He felt his feet leave the ground, then the drone dropped him flat on his back against the cold, metallic table. It fastened him into the restraints, and he felt a robotic arm undoing his pants and yanking them to his feet. Another one pulled down his underwear. He shivered. Steel claws gripped his balls.

"Please--" he choked out. "Not the other one."

"Our orders are for all of them, Citizen Jaylon," the medidrone answered.

His eyes clouded. The machine clamped on to his cold, limp penis. It had retracted into his body as far as it could go, and the drone pulled it out, stretching it to its full length. Metal closed around it.

"It won't hurt a bit," the work drone told him. But the medidrone tightened its grip on his privates, and Jaylon screamed and screamed.

REMADE

I was not born beautiful. Indeed, nothing about me is as ugly and weak as it was when I was a child. Nothing easy to see, anyway.

My mother, on the other hand, was born beautiful. Not just beautiful--perfect, feminine, exquisite. She had the kind of soft skin that made men and women alike long to touch her, and a gentle smile that sent hearts pounding. Even I, who knew how little her true demeanor matched her loveliness, longed for her in a deep, visceral way. I spent my entire youth wondering what it would be like if just once she ran one of her silken fingers along my cheek or pressed her sweet, plump lips to my forehead.

I have never seen my mother smile at me, save once--the most terrifying moment of my life. She did not glare either but curled her lip in elegant distaste every time she looked at my plump, dimpled flesh, my wide owlish eyes hidden behind thick glasses, and my dull, mousy hair.

"It's not even mousy and fine, as I might expect from her father's unfortunate genetics," she explained to her hairstylist, her sharp nails digging into my scalp. "Where did this wild frizz come from? Stringy and matted, more like a rat's fur than human hair."

She gripped my messy ponytail as though she wanted to rip it out by the roots. The stylist nodded and pursed her lips. She doused my scalp in a chemical that stank and burned my eyes. Whatever my mother hoped the treatment would do, it didn't work.

I was eight the first time she took me to a plastic surgeon, the best in the area. The doctor turned out to be a middle-aged woman with a warm, practical expression. I liked her. My mother stared at the tracery of laugh lines on her face and curled her lip.

"What is it that you need, sweetheart?" the doctor asked me. I'd stripped down to a hospital robe, and she looked me over, seemingly oblivious to my hideous body.

Mother sniffed. "Can't you see? She's too fat, for one. And her nose--it's threatening to turn into the same bulbous monstrosity her father had. I'd like it corrected at once. Then we can begin on her jaw line and..."

"I think perhaps there's a misunderstanding," the surgeon interrupted. "I correct birth defects and do reconstructive surgery for children who've been in accidents or other such things. From what I can see, your daughter is a normal, healthy young girl. I would never perform such extensive and unnecessary procedures on a child this young. No respectable doctor would."

"Of course, of course, my mistake. There's plenty of time to correct those things later." My mother smiled at her, charming, but her eyes were like chips of cold blue ice. We left quickly.

I was eleven the next time she took me to a plastic surgeon. This time, she made sure to find someone who wasn't respectable at all. Medvedev had a laboratory and inpatient surgery in a cavernous abode dug out of the side of a mountain.

"Built to withstand bomb," he said as he conducted my mother through endless corridors with smooth rock walls and flickering lights. "I buy from government, cheap."

I shivered. The air was cold and clammy, and the tunnel-like corridors closed in on me. I couldn't breathe, and a wave of vertigo froze me in place.

My mother cursed when I stopped moving. She slapped my flanks as though I was a stubborn donkey. When I still didn't move, she pinched the inside of my arm between her sharp nails and tugged me behind her. I stumbled along, nose running, tears streaming down my face, uglier than usual.

The lab was deep underground. Even the high ceilings didn't prevent me from feeling like an enormous weight of rocks might come crushing down on me any minute. My mother told me to strip off my clothes. I huddled my arms around myself, trembling from cold and embarrassment at having the change in front of a male doctor this time. I left on my underwear at first, but my mother started to pull them down. I struggled against her.

"Don't be stupid, Aura. Dr. Medvedev must examine you thoroughly." She slapped my hands away and tore them off me. "Now get on that table or I'll give you something to cry about." She clicked her nails together menacingly, making a sound like crab claws pinching.

I lay down on the exam table, and they strapped me down, arms and legs spread, every ounce of my quivering, goose-pimpled flesh exposed before them. Medvedev ran a dry, professional hand over the skin of my thigh, and though he didn't hurt me, I shrank away.

"You see what I'm talking about?" My mother said, pointing out parts of my body that were unsatisfactory. "Fat here, blotchy skin everywhere, large pores, nose and chin, and I don't know, everything." She curled her lip and snapped her fingers at me, as though I'd disobeyed her by being born plain and dull.

"I can fix. Technology! We rebuild her completely. There's pain, but must suffer to be beautiful, yes?" He poked my flabby stomach. When I opened my mouth to protest, my mother shoved a gag between my lips.

They left me there, and I heard clickety clack, clickety clack, like hundreds of my mother's nails clicking, coming closer to me all the time. When I saw what they were, my eyes bulged, and I tried to scream.

Spiders--mechanical ones with needle-like legs and stinging syringes. Crawling over my flesh, poking and prodding, sinking their stingers into my exposed body. I struggled against my bonds, whimpering.

"Stop squirming so much, for goodness' sake." My mother's voice, booming and eerie, over an ancient intercom. I spun my eyes around, searching for her, pleading. I saw her through a haze of tears and fogged breath, watching me from an observation deck swathed in glass. Medvedev was beside her, his hands on knobs and buttons, his face red with excitement. He stared down at me as though I was a specimen in a petri dish that he wanted to make wriggle.

"Now, we begin," he said. He pressed a lever. The metal spiders swarmed and plunged their stingers deep into my skin. They injected me all at once, and I burned all over, melting from the inside, pain-maddened. A few torturous seconds later, I finally passed out.

I woke up huddled under a coarse blanket. My mother stood over me, beaming and triumphant. I shivered and pulled the blanket tighter.

"Such improvement!" she gushed, pulling my blanket open and running a cold, smooth hand over my stomach. "All those unsightly bulges are gone--she's not just slimmer, she has more elegant lines!"

She was right. My whole middle felt emptied, as though parts of my flesh had been shaved away. The burning lingered, but beyond that I couldn't find any stitches, or even bruising. The familiar rolls of fat that normally hugged my waist had vanished as if they never existed. It was disconcerting.

"Yes, she is better. More beautiful now," Dr. Medvedev said. He placed a hand on the curve of my back. I clutched the blanket around me once more and shifted uncomfortably.

"You stay here tonight. I check up on her, run tests..." he said.

"Of course," my mother purred. She ran her fingers through the knots in my hair, combing them smooth. She'd never done it so gently before.

Even though the surgery drained me, I was sure I'd never sleep in that place. Medvedev lead me down a narrow hallway, past a series of bolt-locked steel doors.

"Blast proof," he said, tapping the dull metal. "Impossible to break."

The room at the end of the hall had a narrow hospital bed with a thin woolen blanket. It had a tiny attached bathroom that looked spare and clinical. The bed reminded me too much of the exam table he'd strapped me too earlier. It even had restraints on it. Bile rose in my throat.

"You stay here now. Go to sleep." He turned and left before I could say anything. I heard a sharp click. He'd locked the door behind him. I banged on it, panicking.

"Don't leave me in here! I don't want to be alone!" I cried. There was a crackle of static, then his cold voice over the intercom.

"You sleep now. Lights out." Then he plunged me into darkness.

I felt around for that horrible bed, blind in the pitch-black night. No light from the stars or moon or street lamps would ever find its way into that cave. Only a thin line of red emergency light shone under the door. I stared at that red line, trying to decide if it was alarming or comforting, as the only light in the room.

I didn't think I'd fall asleep, but I must have, because I remember waking up. The red line was moving, opening towards me, creeping closer. There's a shadow on the wall shaped like a man. It outlines his lab coat and glasses. I hear him breathing, and cold, dry fingers probing me, touching me. The fingers find the secret parts of my body, the warm parts.

Mother said that last part was just a dream.

We moved into the lab soon after my first "treatment." Mother said it would be better for me, since Dr. Medvedev would be on hand to see to my care. Looking back on it, I wonder if she didn't want anyone else--teachers, nosy neighbors--to notice the dramatic changes in my appearance.

She had decided that paring away my fat wasn't enough. My skin had to go next. It was blotchy and uneven with puberty, and my pores were large and coarse. I don't know what they replaced it with. It had the look and feel of human skin, but a thousand times finer, so smooth it might have belonged to a porcelain doll. Medvedev did a test patch first, and I stared for hours at the contrast between the flawless golden circle on my arm and the goose-pimpled brown skin that surrounded it.

The night before that surgery I had terrible nightmares. I saw them stripping my skin away and feeding it to a thin woman with a perfect complexion and small, sharp teeth. Her eyes were a vivid, poisonous blue, and she watched me hungrily as she ate, licking blood from her face with a delicate pink tongue.

The morning of the surgery I didn't want to fight, but my body refused to listen. I tried to get up, and somehow my legs wouldn't make it over the side of the bed. I couldn't lift my head and my hands clasped convulsively at my old woolen blanket. My mother came to my room when I didn't come down. She clicked her nails impatiently on the metallic frame of my bed. I shuddered. The sound reminded me of Medvedev's mechanical spiders.

"Get up, you lazy girl! What are you still doing in here?" She curled her lip. "Don't you know how lucky you are? You're going to have perfect, flawlessly beautiful skin *forever*. Why, if the procedure goes according to plan, I myself will have the same thing done. But I'm letting you go first, because that's what mothers do." She pinched my cheek between her nails, gouging a chunk out of my soon-to-be-replaced face.

I wanted to do as she asked, but when I tried to move, I felt a warm liquid flowing between my legs. Mother shriveled her nose at the acrid stink of urine. She pounded her fists into my belly and screamed like a savage. Punching, kicking, scratching, venting her rage at me. When she was done, she lifted my chin and stared into my eyes.

115

"You're going to get the surgery," she said, a mad smile stretching across her face. "Because if you don't, I'll leave you here to rot. He'll use you in experiments that will make your hair go white. I'm protecting you, but only if you do what I say."

I nodded silently. The procedure was...worse. When it was done, they left me to recover in the lab, still strapped to the exam table. But something was different. My wrists slipped easily out of the restraints. I felt alive, as though I was wide awake for the first time. My new skin tingled, alert to every subtle change in the air. I ran my fingers over my arms, which were smooth and flawless, not one hair, not one tiny bump or imperfection.

I idly raked my nails down the inside of my arm. It hurt, but the pain was as sharp and crisp as the taste of fresh green apple. Each excruciating cut somehow felt satisfying, even comforting, now that I was the one controlling it. The new skin darkened momentarily, then the scratches knit together and evaporated. There were needles and other more terrifying surgical implements on a table next to me. I dug them into myself, one at a time. My flesh parted beneath the sharp knives, but no matter how long or deep I made the cuts, my skin healed completely in minutes.

My mother found me like that. I heard her coming close, but I didn't move until she laid a hand on my shoulder. I don't know what my face looked like, but when I looked back at her she dropped her hand and stepped back. For the first time I could remember, she seemed uncertain.

"It's time to go back to your room," she told me. I wrinkled my nose. She smelled like sweat and something else that made me feel a bit sick.

"Go on," she said.

I got up, moving towards her. "I want to go home," I said. "I don't want to do this anymore."

"Don't be silly, sweetheart!" she said, fluttering her hands around her. She'd never called me "sweetheart" before. "You've got so much more work to do. Dr. Medvedev has new facial implants, and a muscular net that will keep you toned no matter what you--"

"I want to go home!" I screamed. "RIGHT NOW!"

"Now, darling, if that's what you want, I'll ask the doctor if it's alright."

"He's not a real doctor," I said.

"Of course he is. And you still need care. Come with me now and I promise we'll discuss it more later."

I hesitated, but then she put her soft hand on the back of my neck, rubbing gently. I'd longed for her affection as far back as I could remember. I melted into her touch, not daring to move in case she changed her mind and her loving touch became a blow. After a little while, I followed her to my room, docile as a lamb.

I knew I'd made a mistake when she darted out the door and slammed it shut behind her. I banged against the door, clawing at it until my hands ran red with blood. It didn't matter-- my nails grew back within seconds. So I sat on the floor, rocking back and forth, laughing hysterically, though I wasn't sure what was so funny.

She kept me locked in the room so long I thought she was trying to starve me. There was a sink for water and a toilet for other needs, but no food. Hunger bit deep into my stomach, and I felt dizzy every time I stood up. But the worst part was the lights. Without any outside light, I couldn't tell if it was day or night, or how long it had been since I slept. Or how long I crashed when she finally turned them out.

Sometimes it seemed she only left them on for a couple hours at a time. Other times it felt like I'd been awake for days.

She didn't unlock the door until I was so thin, I could see hollows around the joints of my hands. When she finally came into my room, I wasn't sure if I wanted to cry and beg her forgiveness or spit in her face. Instead, I stared at her, frozen.

"Are you ready to behave?" she asked, hands on her hips.

"Yes," I said, my voice raspy and cracked from lack of use.

"Good," she said. "Then come with me and we'll get some food." She led me down the hall, through a maze of doors I'd never gone past before. We ended up in an elegantly furnished dining room. Medvedev was there, staring at a tablet. He pulled out a chair for my mother and kissed her as she sat down. Me he pinched and poked, pulling on my new skin, lifting my eyelids. When he started to remove the thin hospital gown my mother had hastily thrown over my head, she cleared her throat.

"Ah, yes," he said. "Time for more thorough exam later." A wave of dizziness passed over me, and suddenly the smells of food that filled the room made me nauseated. But my mother spooned some soup into a bowl for me and insisted I eat.

"Well now, after delay we can begin final treatment. First remove fat, next perfect skin, now fix muscle structure." Medvedev waved a hand at me.

"Yes," my mother said. "I want the toning nets for her thighs, abs, and buttocks. As for her face..." She ran a soft finger down my cheek, then dug her nail into the corner of my lip. "Fix that awful expression. A lady should smile

118

sweetly--no glaring, no pathetic mewling looks, no grimaces."

"Yes, I can make face always smile, look natural."

I swallowed a bit of soup, then shut my eyes. I tried very hard to think of nothing at all.

I have no memory of my final surgery. She may have drugged my soup, so I passed out after a few sips. Or perhaps I got painkillers and anesthetic this time. Or maybe my memories of it live in the dark, shut off corners of my brain, and they only awaken in my nightmares.

When I woke up, my mother was there. She had a huge mirror, floor length, and she held it up to me. I had a gentle smile on my lips, and try as I might, I couldn't form any other expression. When I tried to talk, my face felt stiff and tight.

"W-w-w-" I said. My mother laughed, a high tinkling sound, like bells.

"Oh, you'll be able to talk in a little while," she said. "The face net is just a bit tight. I decided I didn't need to listen to any more of your whining."

I wanted to glare at her, but I couldn't. I felt the first touch of madness, as though cold, dark fingers had left shadowy prints on my brain. But when I sat up with unexpected vigor. My mother must have sensed my bewilderment.

"It's the muscular nets," she said. "Your mother knows how to take care of you."

My legs felt strong, powerful. My muscles twitched, as though they were as eager to run. I stretched them out, then leaped off the table. My legs carried me at a speed I'd never imagined I could reach.

"That was fast," my mother said, and her words sounded slow to me, long and drawn out. "Perhaps the Doctor was a little too--" she stopped and stared at me. I had caught one of the doctor's mechanical spiders. It struggled in my hands, and I pulled off its legs, one by one, snapping the thin metal between my fingers like dry twigs.

"That's enough, Aura," she continued. I lashed out at another spider, throwing it against the wall. It smashed into a thousand pieces with a satisfying crunch. Then I thrust a hand through the metal case of a mysterious machine and ripped out a handful of wires.

My mother curled her lip. "Stop that! So immature!"

I stopped.

She held up the mirror and beckoned to me. "Look."

I was taller, shapelier than any normal twelve-year-old. I touched one of my new breasts.

"I had them done now, to spare the bother of another surgery later. Besides, now you're set to earn money for us, my gorgeous girl. We're going to Hollywood after my surgeries." She gazed dreamily at herself in the mirror, lightly touching the fine lines around her eyes.

I didn't want to go to Hollywood, but I didn't say anything. Something else was bothering me.

"Wh-wh-who," I said, "who's going?" I waved my hands in frustration. She finally loved me; I couldn't stand the thought of sharing her.

"Dr. Medvedev, of course. How else was I going to pay him for the work he's done on you? And that he's going to do to me, now that you're finished, and we've discovered the process is safe."

I dug my nails into the palms of my hands, cutting deep into my skin and feeling the tingle as it healed over again. My face twitched with the effort to stop smiling.

"N-n-no, n-n-n-"

120

"Hush now, you ungrateful brat. You owe the doctor everything. He's made you perfect." She pinched my arm with her nails. I tried to grimace, but my face was still in that sweet smile. I hated seeing it in the mirror.

I hated it all. Beautiful, slim, perfect skin, perfect smile. I wasn't me anymore. I tried to feel if any of my original body remained hidden inside me. I felt a thin sliver of vulnerable flesh quivering deep in my chest, aching and human and flawed. I breathed a sigh of relief.

Medvedev stumbled into the lab carrying a bottle of champagne and two glasses.

"Success!" he bellowed. I jumped at the sound of his voice. "Such perfection! Such beauty! Like fairy princess!" He poured a glass of champagne, slopping the alcohol all over the floor. He drank it in a gulp and leaned over my mother, kissing her cheek and neck while she laughed and protested. He poured her a glass, then turned to me, staring at me over the rims of his crooked glasses. I shriveled up, feeling like a rat in an experiment I didn't understand.

My mother pursed her lips. "Aura needs to rest for a bit, Dmitri. Let me take her back to her room."

"She should stay, have fun..." he said.

"She can have her fun later." My mother pulled at my arm to try to lead me away. At first, I thought she was being more gentle than usual, then I realized I was too strong for her to move on her own. After a moment of hesitation, I followed her back to my room. The same one she'd imprisoned me in before. I wondered if I could rip the door off its hinges if she tried that again.

I curled up in bed, suddenly dizzy. Mother pulled the blanket over me. She gave me one of her diet bars, and I devoured it hungrily. I considered asking for more food, but

121

a wave of exhaustion washed over me, until I felt like I could barely move. In my last thoughts, I wondered if she'd drugged the diet bar too.

When I woke, the room was dark, and I was still in my bed. My stomach unclenched. At least I hadn't had another surgery. I heard a metallic click behind me, and I jerked around, staring at the red line beneath the door. It was moving, coming towards me like it had in my dreams. I huddled under my blanket, sick.

Heavy breathing. Footsteps. The sweet smell of champagne. He loomed over me in the dark.

"Beauty, beauty, my sweet creation," he moaned. I heard his pants unzipping.

Panic, panic and sickness--I had to stop him and get away. I scratched at him. My fingers tore into his soft belly as though I'd shoved them into a bowl of warm jello. He shuddered. Sticky warm wetness ran down my arms. Fistfuls of slimy innards in my hands. An awful smell. The heavy body fell to the floor with a dull thud.

I couldn't speak. I couldn't breathe. I felt my mouth and face convulsing, struggling to form an expression of horror, my face frozen in a horrible smile. I gripped the sides of my head and rocked back and forth in a silent scream.

It was still dark. I found the thin line of red light on the floor and felt my way towards it. I stepped on something squishy and unidentifiable, then threw up.

The door was open. I felt my way along the corridor, following a trail of dull red emergency lights. At last I saw a warm glow outlining a door, one with lights on the other side. I knocked.

"Is that you, dearest?" my mother said. I had to hold back tears when I heard her voice. She would help me, she loved me now--she called me "dearest" for the first time. I was too choked up to talk so I knocked again.

"Coming, coming," she said. "Did you lose your key?" She opened the door, and I saw her bathed in golden light.

"M-m-m-mommy," I sputtered.

"Fucking Christ, what are you doing here? Where is Dr. Medvedev?" she said, looking at me and wrinkling her nose. "And what the hell happened to you? Did something go wrong with your surgery after all? Where did all this blood come from?"

"M-m-mommy, p-p-please, he hurt m-m-me..."

"Oh, you stupid girl, don't tell me you've angered the doctor. He never hurt you, or at least only a teeny bit. He only wants you to, well, fulfill his needs. Just be nice--it will be over soon, and he won't have to punish you again."

"P-p-p-please..." I fell on my knees, clinging to her. She stared down at me and narrowed her eyes.

"That's not your blood," she said, her voice strange and quiet.

I shook my head.

"You...you filthy, disgusting, selfish brat!" She slapped me, hard. "You stupid little beast! He was going to fix me, and I'd be beautiful forever, and now you've, you've..." she pounded on me with her fists until I curled up into a ball. "I let you go first, you nasty little bitch, you stinking whore. And now you killed him before he could...just when we knew it was safe and worked..."

"P-p-please, mommy, n-n-n-no more," I pleaded. I caught her hands before she could hit me again. "It hurt...I love you...don't hurt me anymore..."

"I'm done with you, beast. You're on your own. Get the fuck out of my sight."

She struggled, trying to pull away from me. I didn't want to let her go. I loved her. My mommy. I *needed* her. I wrapped my arms around her and held her close, squeezing.

"D-d-don't leave me, mommy. I'll be a g-g-good girl. I'll be beautiful for you, I promise. P-p-please." I held on.

She stopped fighting so much. Then she stopped moving.

She was soft and warm, just like I'd imagined she'd be. We'd never been so close. I snuggled against her, pressing my face into her chest, and closed my eyes. She smelled like her special perfume.

Even when she grew cold and stiff, I didn't let go.

I don't know when the lights went out. I might have fallen asleep again or fainted somehow. When I woke it was dark and cold. I couldn't see my hand in front of my face. I wondered if I could find my way out of the mountain, or if I'd wander around in circles, lost.

I strained my ears, listening for a sound in the darkness. All I could hear was a distant clicking, like a thousand metallic legs scraping against stone.

THE LAST BIRD

Kyrie remembered the day the last bird died. It had been a little brown sparrow with bright black eyes, and it sang in a cheerful whistle. He found it lying on its side, its chest rising and falling in slow, painful gasps, its legs curling beneath it, stiff and pitiful. He cupped it in his hands, feeling each fragile twitch. Its labored breath slowed to a stop, then it grew still. Kyrie felt a shock of numbness, and he held his breath, as though somehow, he could hold it in, hold on to the little bird's life, if only he didn't move or breathe or make a sound.

When he could breathe again, a howl ripped from his throat, desolate and bereft as the north winds his mother had told him about long ago.

Not everyone on Arkship was sad about the bird. "It's no sense to keep them here, anyways," Gardner said. "They eat the seeds we should be storing for arrival. I know everyone liked their singing, but it's better we wait until landing before we take any other eggs out of cryo."

"We could play recorded birdsong in the gardens," Caretaker said. "It soothes people to feel connected with nature."

Kyrie rubbed his toes in the dirt. He wasn't supposed to go barefoot for sanitation reasons, Teacher had constantly reminded him. Or she had, before his parents were lost in the epidemic that swept the ship a few years after takeoff. Now when she looked at Kyrie her eyes watered, and she let him do whatever he wanted. He'd spent most of his school days in the gardens, watching the bird. He didn't think listening to recorded birds singing would be the same. Not at all.

He would have slept in the garden that night if he could. He wanted to bury the bird there, in the shallow soil they used to grow food and produce oxygen. But Gardner frowned and muttered, "Unsanitary," so Kyrie trudged back to his module. He felt strangely heavy, except for the cold, empty hollow in his chest.

He went to school the next day, though he didn't know if it was the right day of the week. Teacher was there, and she looked surprised to see him. The class was much smaller than it used to be before the epidemic. He sat at a table and dug through the paper scraps in the "reusable" bin. There were a few pieces large enough to draw on, and he colored them with the leftover stubs of broken crayons. Red, yellow, green, brown. Blue, like the sky he remembered from a long time ago, before everyone left in the ship. He cut the color paper into squares and folded them into bird shapes, remembering the pattern his dad showed him. He'd never been good at schoolwork, but he knew the shape of things, the way they felt under his fingers.

He stayed until Teacher sent them back to their modules for mealtime. He took the paper birds back with him, but as colorful as they were, they didn't seem alive, even when he hung them up to fly. The air in the ship was motionless except near the vents, so the paper birds just dangled on their strings, still and limp.

He went to school again the next day. Teacher's head rested heavily on her hand, but she gave him a watery smile. But there was no more paper.

"We aren't using paper anymore at all--they want everything digital, using the computers," she told him in a tired voice.

Kyrie's lips trembled, and Teacher added hastily, "I have some scrap metal, foil, bits of wire. They want you kids to learn technology, mechanical things. Could you make your birds out of that? I'll try to help you."

He nodded silently and set to work.

Twelve years after the last bird died, the ship splashed down into an alien sea, then bounced and scraped its way along the coast until the fuselage became wedged into a deep crevice in the sea cliffs. Safety pods and broken off modules lay strewn along the black-sand beach, or else they sank into the water and were lost beneath the waves.

Kyrie's module landed in the water after it broke off the main ship, but its emergency inflatables deployed long enough for a few dazed survivors to scramble to the top of the wreck and stare longingly at the distant shore. Most of them were children.

"It is too far," Teacher said. "Even without fifteen years of muscular atrophy from ship's low gravity. It is too far to swim."

"The water is poison," Caretaker said. "Or it will be if we haven't had the proper immunological supports. We could not survive the native microbiota without developing proper vaccines."

Kyrie said nothing but set to work. In the years since the epidemic, he had built bird after bird, metallic sculptures that moved and flew and sang. He had teased leftover filaments into a vivid array of feathers and sculpted light-weight frames from carbon fibers and nanotubes and scraps of broken metal. No one knew how he'd programmed them, how he'd managed to create the spark of intelligence in their soft black eyes or make them seem to understand him.

No one had bothered about him at all or tried to stop him, and if he was odd and silent at least he stayed out of everyone's way. Besides, the birds were beautiful. The few adults who noticed listened to their songs and watched them fly through the ships and thought their delicate beauty made the days less dreary. The birds followed Kyrie, sometimes flocking around him in a joyous blaze of wings, sometimes trailing behind him like a line of ducklings. It had been so long since they'd seen ducklings.

The flock followed him now, from out of the wreckage, flitting around, beaks open as if to taste the air. They were all different sizes, some as large as ravens with bright coppery legs and soft grey feathers, others as small as sparrows with luminous green wings. The largest was swan-shaped, and its feathers were a shiny metallic color that seemed to shift as it moved--grey, purple, blue, green. This one stayed close to Kyrie and let out a soft, mournful hoot.

Kyrie shook his head at the bird. "No," he said. "It will be all right. What do we have below deck? Ask the little ones to search--they can navigate the small spaces before everything is flooded."

The swan gave a piercing trill, and immediately a handful of tiny metal sparrows flitted into the depths of the sinking module. They pulled up a handful of emergency supplies-- rations, water purifiers, tablets to prevent sickness. The larger birds circled the wreckage, pulling up the torn remnants of the ship's solar sail.

"We could make a sling," Kyrie said. "You could fly us to land, one at a time, if you all pulled together."

The swan hooted again and flapped its wings.

Kyrie did not know how long the birds could carry people before their wings would give out. Many of them were small and fragile, and shore looked far away. And he did not know how long they had before the module slid into the water for good.

"We will do what we can," he said.

Teacher would not go until all the children were safe. These were some of the only children left on board the ship, since most children had grown up since the ship had left, and only a few had been born since then. Kyrie convinced her to leave with the last child, who was very small, so she could hold him on her lap.

"I am so proud of you," she said, as the birds flew her away.

Caretaker was the last person besides Kyrie, but he would not get in the sling. The module was sinking fast. "The ship has been my home," he said, running a hand over the wrecked module. "And now that it's gone, I don't know what to do. I will not leave her now. You go. Otherwise the birds will not have time to save you."

Flying was better than Kyrie had imagined. The air was crisp and clean, and the movement of the wind around him felt like magic after the stagnant air of the ship. So many sights and smells, sensations like he'd never felt.

The swan hooted, questioning.

"Take me someplace where I can look out over the sea," Kyrie said. He did not want to go back just yet and see the people with their sad eyes and their lost friends. But someday he'd find them again, and the birds would sing for them, and perhaps there'd be new birds, living ones rescued and resuscitated from the ship's cryofreeze. This land might even have its own birds, or bird-like creatures, and he would find them and learn what they were like. But if not, he would make more birds for everyone, from the rocks and minerals and metals scattered over the new world. Then he would fill its silences with singing, and its emptiness with joy.

SWAN

Leda had not fit in since the arrival, and her parents worried about her. "You cannot leap from the sea cliffs like that," her mother scolded her. "We do not have enough sterokits to repair any damage you do to your body." She did not add that the colony would not be likely to waste their precious resources on a girl as strange as Leda, but Leda felt the unspoken words.

"You cannot dance alone on the black beach like that," her father said, his face lined and worn. "You should not leave the habitation dome so often. We have so much work to do, and we cannot watch you all the time."

Leda did not know why they needed to watch her outside Dome. She was never alone outside--the birds flew overhead, and everyone knew that the birds were marvels of technology and art, the saviors of the young ones. If they watched over her, what evil could befall her?

Indeed, she felt more danger in the confines of the airless biodome than in the fungal forest or the black beach of Troika. The habitation modules suffocated her, and the maze of tunnels still confused her. But the worst were the other colonists, especially ones near her age she had to see at school or mealtimes. The ones her parents wanted her to bond with.

"I do not understand them," she said of those who were pampered and listless, or who so rarely saw the suns their skin had the pasty, unhealthy pallor of cave dwelling species. She understood others too well. The spoiled ones frightened her. These beloved survivors of the wreck pushed up against the colonies' strictures, and the boldest broke them with alarming arrogance. One of them, Tynd, had trapped her once in a small unused module. He had held her down and laughed at her frantic attempts to escape as she gasped for breath in the confined space. He watched her far too much in school or trainings, and the hungry look in his face made her palms itch.

She tried to tell her parents about Tynd, but they did not hear her. "He is a strong lad," her mother said. "And one of the few procreators in your generation. You cannot afford to be picky, or you will risk the colony."

Leda frowned at the word "procreator." She wanted to know what it meant, but her mother gave evasive answers.

That night Leda slipped from the biodome to spend the night in the fungal forest, looking up at the stars. They had all come from out there, she knew, though she had few memories of their previous planet. She remembered Ship, the gargantuan structure whose remains formed the basis of the biodome. Ship had had gardens and living quarters and labs, like Dome, but then the Birdmaker had walked among the people. She remembered him, shy and quiet, his creations trailing behind him in a marvelous riot of color. He had been a boy then, a few years older than her, and he didn't notice her watching him.

Few had seen him since the landing so many years ago, though his birds still flew overhead near Dome. There was one near her now, singing as it sat on the cap of one of the tallest fungi in the forest. She sang in answer.

The air was hazy and silver from the bursts of spores released by the enormous, treelike fungi. A light wind made their spires and soft gills wave, so that they looked like the underwater creatures she'd seen on videos of the Earth's oceans. In the soft light of the twin moons, the colors of their caps glowed-- iridescent blues, silvery purples, luminescent oranges.

The elders longed for the homeworld, but Leda loved Troika. She loved the musky-sweet scent of the forest spores, and the glorious nights of the triple moons. She loved the soft carpet of blue-green moss on the forest floor, and the gentle brushes of blood ferns on her legs. But most of all she loved the freedom of being able to escape, to get away, to be alone, which she had never known before they landed. She did not understand why so many people stayed huddled up in Ship's corpse.

She waited until the rise of the third moon before heading back, even though it meant she'd have to struggle to stay awake during training.

The dome was silent during her return, with no one awake but the security drone. It blinked at her in admonishment but gave no alarm. She had almost made it to her sleeping module when she heard a noise behind her. She glanced back, expecting to see a cleansing drone making its nightly rounds through the halls. But instead she saw a flash of red and heard the hollow thud of footsteps. Someone else was awake. Who?

She started to walk towards the sound, then stopped, afraid. She hurried to place her palm on the identilock to her module and rushed inside when it opened. As the doors closed behind her, she thought she heard footsteps and ragged breathing. There was a door cam outside her module, and she pulled it up on her wall screen. Tynd. He was leaning against the outside of her module, out of breath, his face flushed.

So close, she thought. They were separated by less than a centimeter of polymers. Much less. Even though she knew he couldn't hear or see her, Leda froze. Tynd grinned at the door cam, and it felt like he was staring straight at her.

"Nearly caught you," he said. "You shouldn't be out of your module so late." He caressed her module door with disturbing possessiveness.

Leda did not sleep until a long while after he'd left. When she woke in the morning, she waited until she saw others rushing about their morning duties on her door cam before she dared unlock her module.

She arrived at her assigned training a few minutes late and discovered to her dismay that she wouldn't be working in the Mycelium Lab. Instead a group of female trainees, including her, had been summoned to the audience room for "announcements and the delineation of additional duties." Something about those words bothered Leda. She walked to the assigned room as though she had magnetic traction in her shoes.

"Cheer up," a builder said as she passed by him. "It's not like it's all bad." He smirked and made a hooting sound. Leda's face grew hot.

The audience room was large by some standards, but it still felt close and hot and confining. Leda sat at the back close to the doors. She could hardly breathe.

The new Caretaker was an older woman with calculating eyes and a cold, hard-bitten smile. She approached the pedestal with grim, determined cheer.

"You are all so blessed," she began. "You survived our long journey and our terrifying plummet from space." There was a smattering of applause, but it died quickly.

"So many of us suffered then, and in the long years after, struggling to build our dream, our colony. And by the time we noticed that the journey and the crash had taken a terrible toll on our health and our fertility, it was too late to repair the damage."

There were a few murmurs in the group now. Leda glanced towards the doors behind her. They were closed, and a security drone patrolled them. Her head felt like it was floating. She tried to breathe, but the hot air choked her.

"But we had hope," the Caretaker continued, "in each of you, and in select males as well. We monitored you and to our great joy, discovered that each of you has developed properly, as healthy as any Earth girl."

Leda shifted from side to side, rocking uneasily in her seat. I'm too young, she thought. But she knew she was of age--her initial training was coming to an end, and she would be expected to choose a specialization or an apprenticeship soon. Would she feel so young, so unprepared, if she could choose a man she desired? She thought of her youthful crus+h on Kyrie, the Birdmaker. He'd had a gentle soul, and clever fingers, and a quick intelligence that gleamed out of his dark eyes even when he stumbled for words. She would have not felt so afraid if he was here.

But Kyrie was not here, and only a handful of males from her age group were in the auditorium. She looked them over--most were harmless, skinny boys who blushed and bumbled and stared at their feet when they tried to talk to girls. But Tynd was there, and he did not blush. He stared at her and she wanted to flee.

Tears pricked her eyes. She glanced back at the security drone. There was no escape, not today.

Caretaker continued talking, and Leda could barely hear her through the tumult in her head. Assignments, ceremonies, hand-fastenings. Hormone monitoring and ultrasounds. Possible egg extractions, to guarantee the survival of their gametes as a backup.

"There are...scenarios...we have considered but hope to avoid," the older woman droned on.

Finally, there were letters, in red and gold envelopes.

"For good luck," Caretaker said, smiling now. "And to make it more--romantic--than simply updating your computer records."

One of Caretakers attendants passed out the letters. Leda thought she might throw up when an elderly colonist pressed her letter into her hands, smiling warmly. She hadn't used actual paper in years, and the envelope felt luxurious and forbidden all at once, a heavy seal on a fate she did not desire. She opened it gingerly, as though it might bite her. The paper inside was covered in numbers--a chart of dates, hormone levels, and at the very bottom, an ID number for the male she'd been assigned. Tynd.

The paper fluttered out of her hands to the floor, like a bird with a broken wing.

That night Leda huddled on the bed in her module. She wanted to go to the seashore and watch the waves, which at this time of year glowed with delicate bioluminescence. But Tynd had waited for her the night before, and she did not want to see him again while she was alone and vulnerable. He had followed her after the announcements in the auditorium, chasing after her and trying to catch her arm. She lost him in the crowd and rushed back to her module, where she would be safe.

Safe. For how long? Ship's walls were closing in on her, crushing her tiny module, slowly, inexorably. The ceremony would be in six weeks, and then it would be over. He would have her; the colony would deliver her to him to bear his intimacies and his children. And there was no telling how long she would have to endure it, or if it would eventually end and she would be set free.

She shuddered. I must get out, she thought. If only for a little while. There were footsteps in the hall. They stopped in front of her module entrance. She did not dare look at the feed for the door camera but checked and rechecked her secure-lock. She must get out, she thought again, burying her head in the worn sleep-sack she'd used since before landing. But not tonight.

Leda woke early the next morning, so she could slip down to the beach. A faint glow of pink and green luminescence was still visible along the black sands. A single pale moon, Wilusa, still hung in the sky, but her silvery light dimmed as the great star Dardan rose to take her place.

She kicked off her boots. The sand was cool beneath her feet, then the water gave her a bracing chill. She ignored the prickly cold, wading into the shallows. Sea lotus stems undulated beneath the waves, their curling tendrils heavy with oblong fruits.

We should harvest them soon, she thought. She'd have to do it herself--the elders were suspicious of native fruits and often neglected to collect them, despite the colony's scarce resources.

Leda heard joyful whistles coming from the nearby bluffs, and she looked up. Birds, a chorus of them, these ones wearing lustrous purple and green feathers. They spread their wings as though to wave to her. There was so much artistry in their delicate circuits that she could not tell if the filigree was functional or for beauty. She waved back. The flock took to the air and circled around her, singing. One landed on her hand and cocked its head. It made a gentle hoot, as though to encourage her.

Leda sat down on the sand, and the electric bird hopped onto her out-stretched knee. She rubbed her eyes, which were bloodshot and itchy from crying and a lack of sleep. She took a deep breath and gazed out at the sea. It calmed her.

"They are going to make me...breed...with a man I despise," she said, her voice hoarse. "I don't want to breed, at least not with him. I'm--afraid."

The bird gave an indignant chirp, as though it understood her and sympathized. At its signal, the flock clustered around her, hooting. Soft feathers brushed her fingertips. What did he make them from, she wondered? Mycelium filaments? The soft, downy fluff that carried spores on the wind? He had once used carbon nanotubes, she knew, but how could he make those now without the colony's resources?

Perhaps he has died, she thought, and these are the last of his creations. Her insides quailed, and her breath quickened. The quiet boy. She had cared about him.

She forced herself to ask. "What happened to your creator? Is he still alive?"

The lead bird chirped and bobbed its head. Yes, she thought, and her breath came easier. "Is he lonely, where he is? Or is he happy living with just you?"

The bird flapped its wings once, and she wondered if it was unsure how to answer.

"If he'd ever like to talk to a person, he could talk to me," she said. "I'll keep his secrets. I won't try to make him come back if he doesn't want to."

The flock cooed softly to themselves, as if conversing. For all she knew, they were conversing. The children of the colony had thought the birds were not controlled or automated, but true AI. But elders scoffed. Even as great a talent as the Birdmaker could not have created an AI with the meager resources he had at his disposal, they said. He'd never been given anything but scraps, even before the crash. But Leda could see the exquisite mechanical subtlety of his creations, their vigor, their independent spirits, and she thought the children were right.

The lead bird chirped loudly, as if bringing the others to attention. They stopped cooing, bobbed their heads at Leda, and flew away in a graceful arc over the top of the bluffs. The lead bird was the last to leave, and it circled her head once, as if to reassure her.

Leda stayed on the beach a few moments more, basking in the light of the great star and allowing its rays to warm her. She never felt like this onboard Ship or in Dome. She wished she could catch the rays in her hand and carry them with her for luck and courage. But she could not. Instead, she trudged back the way she'd come, up the path to Dome, the place she stayed that never felt like home.

Her parents waited anxiously outside her module. "Where have you been?" her mother said. "We were told you--did not take the news of your...assignment...well."

Her father hugged her with one arm but did not meet her eyes. "Tynd will not let you continue to run about like this," he said, his voice rough and cracked. "That would be well for you."

"Do not speak his name to me," Leda said. "I—I—"

Her mother clasped her hand and shushed her. "We do not have to discuss him, but there are arrangements to be made. Appointments with the Caretaker and the medical team that you must undergo. A ceremony to plan."

"I do not want a ceremony," Leda said.

"Hush. There must be a ceremony. The elders insist upon it. Yours is scheduled in six weeks' time."

"So soon..."

"It was the time chosen. Come quickly, we must..."

But Leda shook her head no. "I am tired, and I must sleep." She was tired--she had not slept the night before. But the thought of planning a ceremony to celebrate her assignment to Tynd made her feel ill.

"But you must decide where to have it, at the very least," her mother persisted. "Perhaps the auditorium?"

"No." Leda covered her face with her hands and tried to think. "Outside. On the beach, near the sea." At least it would calm her.

"Outside?" her mother's mouth looked pinched.

"If that is what you wish," her father interjected, "then we will see it done."

Leda nodded and at last they let her go. She made it back to her module and collapsed into her sleeping sack.

She was not allowed to escape her duties for the next few weeks. She was ordered to the medical bay almost daily where a team of techs subjected her to a series of examinations.

"Healthy body, few if any markers for genetic defects," a masked tech said. "Correct hormone levels and high probability of successful conception should she be bred immediately after the ceremony."

"Where is she on her cycle?"

"Close to ovulating, well developed gametes."

"Schedule an egg withdrawal. We can use her gametes for one of the others."

That was painful, though the techs insisted it would not be. There was a large needle, long and glistening, and she sobbed when she learned where they would stick it. She covered her face with her hands and tried to relax as they asked her to. Afterwards, her belly cramped, and her hidden parts were sore and aching. Her mother had taken her back to her module.

"There aren't many choices for the ceremonial dress, which must be white. On Earth, there were endless shops and you could search for days, weeks, months even," her mother sighed. She held a short pamphlet which she showed to Leda as though offering her a treat.

"Pick whatever you'd like," Leda said. "I don't care."

Her mother frowned. "I wish you would stop sulking. It's not all bad, you know. He's brash and headstrong, to be sure, and perhaps over-aggressive, but at least he's well-formed. And he has a strong genetic makeup. You should be honored."

"He is not my choice."

"We are too far from Earth to afford you the luxury of choices."

"It was not my choice to make the journey either."

Her mother slapped her, hard, across her face. "You are here now, and you will do what is best for you."

Leda's cheek stung, and part of her wanted to dissolve into tears. But somehow the soreness of her body and the sharp pain on her face suffused her with rage.

"You do not know what is best for me! None of you!" she said through gritted teeth. Her mother grabbed her arm, but Leda pushed passed her, anger giving her strength despite her aching body. She ran through the warren of Dome's tunnels, searching for an escape. A few people called after her, but she refused to stop. At last she found an outside door. She stepped through quickly and closed it behind her.

It opened on the forest. She breathed in the scent of fresh green ferns and the earthy, musky scent of the towering fungi. It was late afternoon and the air was warm. Insects hummed, and Leda could hear the soft clicking of the climbing crabs as they scampered over the fungi's spires.

Her head swirled, and she felt faint from running so soon after the procedure. She wondered a little way into the forest then sank into a soft clump of ferns. A trio of fungi shaded her with their vivid purple-gold caps. The sky had the clear blue brightness of early afternoon. The great star Dardan reached its apex and glowed golden and beautiful. The lesser star, Agon, had risen just above the tallest fungi. Leda's breathing slowed as she watched the clouds in the sky drift overhead.

Her mind drifted. Slowly, she became aware of something sitting near her, not disturbing or disrupting her, but quietly waiting for her awareness. Her eyes refocused and she let her reverie slip away with only a touch of reluctance.

The quiet being near her was a bird, or at least shaped like one. It had a long graceful neck that curved into a proud arch. Its feathers were deep black and shined with reflected rainbows from the fungi. It was larger than any of the other birds she'd seen so far.

"Who are you?" she asked. She knew without a doubt that this creature was no automaton, but a true AI, a living mind.

"I am Swan," the mechanical bird said. "He asked me to find you if I could. He monitors the colony's emergency communications network, and he became alarmed when they could not find you."

"They're looking for me?"

"Yes." Swan did not elaborate, but cocked its head, as though listening to something she could not hear. "I could let them know you are safe." The AI bird did not elaborate, but she heard its unspoken question.

Leda sighed. "I'll have to go back."

"Yes," Swan said. "But not right away."

She lifted her head, and her heart thrummed in her ears like the rhythmic hum of the colony's beehives. "Could you take me to him?"

Swan listened again, then nodded. "Yes."

"Then let's go."

"As you wish." Swan unfolded its wings, and Leda gasped at their full glory, which stretched further than she'd thought. One powerful beat, and the mechanical bird was in the air. She followed it, wandering deeper into the fungal forest than she'd ever ventured before. Farther than anyone else in the colony had ever gone, she thought, besides the Birdmaker himself. After a few miles, the forest opened to a great expanse of sky. She stood on a tall cliff overlooking a tiny bay. She wondered if it was cloaked somehow or if it was just remote enough that the colony hadn't found it.

There was a young man sitting in a flat stretch of rock nearby. He had shaggy hair now, and even a scraggly beard, but when he looked up from the wires and bits of fiber he was turning over in his fingers, she knew him.

"Kyrie," she said. "The Birdmaker. You are here."

He stood up and smiled at her. His smile looked awkward and rarely used. "So are you."

They talked for a while after that, and he showed her all his creations, at least, he said, smiling bashfully, those that were finished and worth showing. She told him about her training, at first, but as he listened with kindness and patience, she told him more.

"The truth is...I do not fit in there. And I don't know if I even want to fit in. I like who I am, but..." Leda stopped. She could not say the rest of it, to mention the ceremony to him, or the dreaded breeding. His eyes were so gentle and warm, and she saw so much of the boy she'd once admired from afar in his gaze. She could not tell him about such a sordid, ugly thing.

Kyrie put his arm around her, and if his gesture was awkward and unsure it was also simple and heartfelt, and she liked it. She held his hand. It was warm and brown from the sun, and his fingers were long and clever. They held each other until Dardan began to sink beneath the horizon.

Leda sighed. "I must get back," she said.

"If you would like--" Kyrie began. He looked away, then back at her. "You are welcome to come back," he finished softly. "I like living here, but I am... lonely. And you are nice to be around."

144

"I will," she said. "I will come back."

"Just ask the birds," he said, "and they will show you the way."

He walked with her back to Dome, and Leda lingered by the entrance, reluctant to go in. She looked up at Kyrie. Standing up, he was taller than her, long and lanky. She stood close to him. He brushed strand of her hair away from her face, then leaned down and kissed her. Her heart fluttered, and she reached her arms around his neck.

There was a loud clang as one of Dome's outer hatches lifted. Leda let go of Kyrie, startled. Fluorescent lights and the hum of electrical circuits overwhelmed her, and someone pulled her inside. She blinked, uncertain.

Caretaker and her assistants stared down at her. A large male had his hands clamped on her arms.

"Did you lie with him?" Caretaker asked. "Did you attempt to procreate with an unassigned male?"

Leda shook her head, but Caretaker bore down on her, glaring.

"You will not attempt to see him or to leave Dome again," Caretaker said. "We have carefully selected a mate for you based on your genetic profile. You will have a high probability of success with Tynd, not just with conception, but in producing desirable genetic traits. The Birdmaker's genetic profile was lost in the landing. Your reproductive success with him is highly unpredictable and therefore a risk to the colony and its resources. And..."

Caretaker hesitated, then bared her teeth in a tight smile. "Tynd is my son. He desires you, and you will make him happy."

"I do not desire him, nor do I wish to procreate with him," Leda said. She tried to wriggle away from the man holding her, but he gripped her so tightly his fingers left red marks in her flesh. She winced.

"Surely Tynd is a genetic match with other girls!" she cried. "Let him be satisfied with one of them."

"As a matter of fact, he is not," Caretaker said. "But that is beside the point. You are to do as directed, or there will be consequences." She hit Leda in the face again and again, until Leda's ears rang and her eyes began to swell shut.

"You are confined to your module for three days without rations. If you are caught leaving Dome before the ceremony, the consequences will be severe and painful."

Leda did not mind at first that they had locked her in her module. It was hers, and she had often retreated there when she'd needed to escape the antiseptic bustle of the other colonists. True, they had cracked her head against the door as they shoved her in, and Caretaker's eyes had a malicious glint as she'd changed the door code to prevent Leda's escape, but things could be worse. At least here she was safe from Tynd, and she could close her eyes and see Kyrie the Birdmaker, feel his lips on hers.

But she had grown too tall to even stand upright in module, and as she lay there hour after hour, the tumult in her mind kept her from sleep. The walls seemed to close in, smothering her. When she'd felt like that before, she could escape to the outside, to the forest or the sea.

Now there was no escape. Worse, the way out seemed to her to be closing, not just for the few days of confinement, but for her life. She'd never escape Tynd after the ceremony. She'd be trapped in Dome, in the colony, in the mating and breeding modules. They'd never let her out again. She'd never see Kyrie, or his beautiful birds, or the forest she loved.

146

She had to force herself to breathe, to remind herself that she still could breathe, to keep herself from panicking.

Her parents came on the eve of the third day to let her out. Leda watched them on the monitor, fumbling with Caretaker's code, her mother's lips pinched and tight, biting and chewing on the words she planned to say. But when the door opened, Leda fell forward into their arms, blinded with tears. Her mother's mouth fell open and her angry words spilled harmlessly on to the ground.

"She is ill," Leda heard her mother say. "They should not have...not so soon after the egg extraction..."

"Shh," her father said. "It's best we just get her something to eat, let her walk around a little while, get a breath of fresh air..."

"But we cannot allow her to--"

"We can take her to the gardens. It's better there."

It was better there--she could smell the earth and the air was fresher. Leda let them coax her to eat as she stared at the stunted Earth trees, so small and weak compared to the great forest outside. Had they forgotten? she wondered. Had they become so accepting of their limited habitat that they could not leave it even if their cage door was opened? Would she become like them someday? She blinked, trying to make her mind work again.

"The ceremony," she said. "Will it still be outside?"

Her mother would not meet her eyes. "We discussed it with the Caretaker, and she felt, under the circumstances..."

"If it is not outside, I will not go. I will scream and fight if they try to take me. I would rather die."

Her father patted her gently, and she tried not to flinch when he accidentally brushed the bruises Caretaker's agent had left on her arm. "We can talk to her. She's not completely unreasonable, and since you so greatly wish it..."

"I do." There would be no way to contact him before the ceremony, she thought. He wouldn't know about it--she hadn't told him. But he could see her one last time, or his birds could, and somehow, she might be able to send a message. Somehow.

"The ceremonial dresses. I would look at them again."

"Of course," her mother said. She gave Leda a quivering smile and pulled up the catalogue on her tablet. Leda swiped through them. White ribbons, beads, puffs of cloth. And on one of the last ones, lace that looked like feathers. She made her choice.

The next day, Leda discovered that Caretaker had also re-assigned her to ship construction and maintenance, one of the most undesirable apprenticeships among the youth of the colony. Leda missed her assignment in the Mycelium lab--she'd developed a deep understanding and knowledge of Troika's great fungi, surpassing even her mentor. But the maintenance engineer was an elderly, soft-spoken man who allowed her free use of the colony's equipment, leftover parts, and broken drones, and that suited her well for now.

"The best way to learn is by doing," he said. "There are broken things. Try to fix them."

"I will," she said. He nodded gravely, as if he understood all the words she'd left unspoken.

She did not have any great mechanical understanding--her passion was for the forest, not machines--but Leda did have patience, steady hands, and strong motivation. And in the weeks before her ceremony, the project she'd envisioned took shape. Not a perfect, sleek shape, but a recognizable shape forged from a tiny maintenance drone and feathery lace. As the ceremony grew closer, she worked late into the night, sometimes even falling asleep in the machine shop. At least Tyn did not think to look for her there.

The morning of the ceremony, she woke in a cold sweat. The project was finished, but she would not have time to test it, and she did not know if it would be enough. But it was all she had. She clutched it in clammy hands and hurried to her module, where her mother would arrive soon to take her for the ritual cleansings.

"Your eyes are puffy and red," her mother clucked after she arrived. "And your hair smells like industrial solvents." Leda shrugged and allowed her mother to herd her through the preparations, keeping her project hidden in a voluminous pocket. The dark circles under her eyes were concealed with flesh-tone paints, and her pallor disguised with rouge. Her hair was twisted into a nest of braids.

While her mother bickered with Caretaker's assistants about timing and other ceremonial details, Leda slipped her project out of her pocket. It appeared to be an ornament--an elegant dove with lacy wings. She nestled it into her hair, where it would be hidden beneath her veil for most of the ceremony.

The rest of the day passed in a blur. Leda complied with her mother's instructions as best she could to avoid suspicion, but her mind drifted to the dreaded events before her. Her stomach gave queasy lurches every time she imagined the potential consequences of failure. Life with Tynd, perhaps after being horribly re-conditioned. Being trapped in the colony, away from the forest she had grown to love. She could hardly breathe the stifling, recycled air any longer. She swayed on her feet, and her mother demanded she sit down and eat a meal packet.

At last it was time. Her mother and father lead her outside, and Leda could feel the breeze for the first time in weeks. Even through her veil, she could smell the sweet-musk of the silver spores. She had come alive again, as though she'd emerged from under the ground like the first tendrils of a new fern. The veil obscured her sight, but she could hear people around her--nervous shuffling, bated breath. Her parents lead her towards the beach. As they approached, their grip on her arms loosened, their hands becoming slippery with seat.

Were they nervous? Exhausted from the walk? Or was it something else--shame or hesitance at giving her to a man she hated? Leda did not know, but as their hold on her weakened, her steps gained strength. Even blinded her feet knew the path she walked better than they did.

They stopped walking, and she heard Tynd's heavy breathing and felt the weight of him in front of her. Thick hands fumbled with her veil, and as it lifted, she closed her eyes to spare herself the sight of him for a moment longer. She reached up her hand, as though to arrange a misplaced braid, and her fingers found the trigger on her dove. She felt it lift into the air with a mournful cry, and she opened her eyes.

Tynd's face was red and sweating, and his eyes were squeezed into an angry squint. Caretaker was yelling, her finger pointing. Leda's dove cried again, haunted keening transforming into a joyful call. More birds rose into the air from the surrounding cliffs, blending their voices into a wild chorus that drowned out the shouting around her.

Rough hands grabbed at her and clutched her ceremonial dress, but Leda ripped herself free. She ran down the beach, more sure-footed on the soft sand than the other colonists. The birds circled her, batting their wings at her pursuers.

But she could not run forever--her confinement in Dome had weakened her. The Caretaker's man, the large one, caught her veil in his fist, jerking her head back. She could feel herself losing her balance, struggling to keep running. She threw up her hands to steady herself, hoping for a miracle. And caught hold of something--a mechanical leg, ridged enough to give her a good grip. The black swan.

It flapped its wings and hoisted itself higher, trying to pull her up. But Leda could hear its mechanisms grinding, and knew it was not strong enough to lift them both. She kicked wildly at Caretaker's man, who now was gripping her skirts. A flurry of birds swarmed his face. She kicked again, harder this time, and felt her ceremonial gown rip. She propelled herself away. And then she saw a second swan, one which she had never seen before.

The new swan was as shimmering white as the other was black, as white as the glint of sunlight off the afternoon clouds. Its powerful wings beat at the Caretaker's man, and it snaked its long neck forward to bite his arm. He yelped and let Leda go. She reached up with her free hand and grasped its leg. Then she was flying, soaring over the waves.

The swans' wings extended, their mechanical feathers growing and shaping themselves to give them better lift. The webbing around their feet extended over her hands and wrists to hold her securely in place. She had never seen them do that before and wondered if Kyrie had developed the tech recently. Neither swan spoke.

They flew her along the coast, then swooped into a sheltered bay. They circled lower, coordinating their flight until the ocean spray tickled Leda's toes. They set her down in the shallow water, cushioning her landing. Her shoes had fallen off at some point in her journey, and her feet sank in the soft black sand. The tattered pieces of her torn skirt undulated in the water like the arms of a sea creature.

She waded to shore. Kyrie was there, climbing down the steep bluffs. She watched him gracefully navigating the rocky cliff, until he reached the sand. Their eyes met across the beach. His gaze made Leda forget her cold feet and bedraggled dress, her exhaustion. Warmth suffused her limbs. They ran to each other and felt the joy of each other's kiss.

The white swan landed beside Leda. She knew he had built it for her to be her own bird companion, a match for his magnificent black one. The two swans, black and white, stood near them, and their necks stretched into graceful arches, beaks touching in an intimate gesture. Leda looked up at Kyrie's gentle smile and for the first time she could remember, she felt at home.

ACKNOWLEDGMENTS

Thank you to everyone who inspired, encouraged, and helped me to write this book.

Thank you in particular to my beta readers, Sarah Mensinga, Gerardo Delgadillo, and of course, my mother Kristine Lantgen. Your feedback was so helpful in the creation of this book.

Thanks as well to all the members of my writing group: Dani Baxter, Diana Beebe, Mervyn Dejecacion, Sean Easley, Kellie Patrick-Getty, Holly Rylander, and Jared Pope. You kept me writing when I got discouraged and gave me so much help and encouragement.

Special thanks to my husband David Farmer for creating such a beautiful book cover. Your support has been invaluable, and I'm so amazed by your talent and creativity. I'm thankful every day for our beautiful family.

AUTHOR BIO

Alexis Lantgen is a writer, teacher, and classical musician. She loves Renaissance Faires and all things science fiction and fantasy. Her short stories have appeared in the Gallery of Curiosities, Phantaxis, Red Sun Magazine, and Swords and Sorcery Magazine. Her nonfiction articles have appeared in Renaissance Magazine. Alexis is occasionally on twitter @TheWiseSerpent and has been spotted once in a blue moon on Instagram. She lives with her husband, her two beautiful, spirited children, and two very patient cats in Texas.

FORTHCOMING

Lunarian Press is pleased to announce that Alexis Lantgen's next book, a collection of Fantasy short stories titled *Saints and Curses*, will be released in the Spring of 2019. For updates on more fantastic fiction, author events, calls for submissions, and more:

VISIT OUR WEBSITE

www.lunarianpress.com

FOLLOW US ON TWITTER

@LunarianPress

LIKE THE AUTHOR ON FACEBOOK

@alexislantgenauthor

EMAIL US

lunarianpressbooks@gmail.com

Made in the USA
Middletown, DE
16 June 2020